I0784322

THUG ME THE RIGHT WAY 2

NAI

URBAN AINT DEAD

URBAN AINT DEAD
P.O Box 448
Maybrook, NY 12543

No part of this book may be reproduced or transmitted in any form by any means, electronic or mechanical, including photocopying, recording, or by any information storage system, without written permission from the publisher.

Copyright © 2024 By Nai

All rights reserved. Published by URBAN AINT DEAD Publications.

Cover Design: P. Wise / The Wise Services

URBAN AINT DEAD and coinciding logo(s) are registered properties.

No patent liability is assumed with respect to the use of information contained herein. Although every precaution has been taken in the preparation of this book, the publisher and the author assume no responsibility for errors or omissions. Neither is any liability assumed for damages resulting from the use of the information contained herein. This is a work of fiction. Names, characters, places, and incidents are either the product of the author's imagination or are used fictitiously. Any resemblance to actual events, locales, or persons living or dead is entirely coincidental.

Contact Author on FB: Authoressnai / IG: @authoressnai / TikTok: @authoressnai / Website: hoodloverssociety.com / Email: hoodloverssociety@gmail.com

Contact Publisher at www.urbanaintdead.com

Email: urbanaintdead@gmail.com

ISBN: 979-8-9902387-6-3

CONTENTS

SOUNDTRACKS

Scan the QR Code below to listen to the Soundtracks/Singles of some of your favorite U.A.D titles:

Don't have Spotify or Apple Music?
No Sweat!
Visit your choice streaming platform and search URBAN AINT DEAD.

Currently on lock serving a bid?
JPay, iHeartRadio, WHATEVER!
We got you covered.

Simply log into your facility's kiosk or tablet, go to music and
search URBAN AINT DEAD.

URBAN AINT DEAD

Like & Follow us on social media:
FB - URBAN AINT DEAD
IG: @urbanaintdead
Tik Tok - @urbanaintdead

SUBMISSIONS

Submit the first three chapters of your completed manuscript to <u>urbanaintdead@gmail.com</u>, subject line: Your book's title. The manuscript must be in a .doc file and sent as an attachment. The document should be in Times New Roman, double-spaced, and in size 12 font. Also, provide your synopsis and full contact information. If sending multiple submissions, they must each be in a separate email. Have a story but no way to submit it electronically? You can still submit to URBAN AINT DEAD. Send in the first three chapters, written or typed, of your completed manuscript to:

URBAN AINT DEAD

P.O Box 448

Maybrook, NY 12543

DO NOT send original manuscript. Must be a duplicate.
Provide your synopsis and a cover letter containing your full contact information.
Thanks for considering URBAN AINT DEAD.

AUTHOR'S NOTE

I love what I do and even when things don't go exactly the way I plan, it doesn't stop the passion behind this pen. It also helps that I'm a beast wit this shit. NEVER let anything pull you away from your purpose & NEVER miss an opportunity to POP YO SHIT! It's yo right of passage baby. Muah, THE HOOD LOVE DEALER

Maine

Watching Kaia's back as she walked off the visiting room floor had me feeling like asshole of the year. I wanted so bad to run after her, but I was stuck. This shit was all bad. And although I could explain why Kandice was sitting across from me with a baby in her hands, I knew that no explanation would make sense to Kaia. I'd just set us back a few steps in our relationship. And at this juncture, in our current fragile state, we couldn't afford that. Not only did Kaia's heartbroken face fuck my head up, but the small belly formed underneath her hoodie made my heart skip a beat.

I replayed our daily conversations in my head to see if I had missed any hints and came up blank. She'd done a helluva job keeping her pregnancy a secret. Part of me was blowed, but the other part that had come to love everything about Kaia, I smiled big at the thought of her carrying my seed. First born came to my mind, but that seemed like the furthest thing from reality with Kandice sitting in front of me with her baby and her face turned up.

"What were you saying again?" I finally snapped out of my daze now that Kaia was no longer in sight.

"Oh, now you remember that me and your son are sitting here?" She twisted her neck and popped her lips.

"Look, I didn't ask you to bring the lil' one here. Hell, I didn't even ask you to come, so you can chill the fuck out with the neck rolling. You look dumb as hell. And stop calling him my son, we don't know that yet." She was pissin' me off with that shit. Since she had sat down ten minutes ago, she kept on with the, *your son this, your son that.* As far as I was concerned, the only parent lil' man had was her until the DNA test proved he was mine.

"So, your bitch pops up with half a belly and all of a sudden he's not your baby? You got me fucked up if you think I'ma bout to be a single mother."

"No, *you* got you fucked up. The difference between you and Kaia, other than the obvious, is I made love to her *raw*. I fucked you with a condom that I'm positive you tampered with. And he's been **not** my baby since **you** decided to keep him. You keep calling my girl out her God given name and I'ma let her people loose on you."

I didn't give a fuck about Kandice's feelings, and she needed to understand that. If her son turned out to be mine, it was because she trapped me. I couldn't help but to sneak a peek at the baby when she first came in. To me, he didn't have any features yet. She swore up and down that he looked just like me though.

I watched as he stirred and began to cry a little. Kandice looked up and stretched out her arms to hand him to me. My hands remained folded on the table, making no attempt to reach over. Sucking her teeth, she rolled her eyes before pulling him back to her chest again. I wasn't holding or getting attached until I knew for sure that he was mine. Call me fucked up if you want, I was veering on the side of caution. His cries made me think about the baby Kaia was carrying, our baby. Klein had to get me up outta here asap.

"Look, I'ma go. Don't pop up here no more. I can get my lawyer to have me swabbed while I'm in here and we can get answers. Until then, don't reach out to me and don't fuck with my girl. You don't wanna test me on that." I knew I had read her mind because she rolled her eyes when I said it.

"I don't give a damn about her or her baby. We can do ya little test, but when it comes back that you're the father, don't run and hide. You're gonna be apart of our lives." She covered the baby's head in the blue blanket, grabbed her bag, and left.

Kandice was determined to give me hell. Ant's baby mother didn't have nothing on her vindictive ass. But the difference between me and Ant was, I wasn't bout to play the "crazy baby mother" bullshit with her if the baby turned out to be mine. I would have Kandice fucked over and raise my son as a single father in a heartbeat.

I had to get up from the table to avoid catching a valid charge for yoking her stupid ass up. The guard looked at me with a smirk before opening the door and handing me off to head back to my cell. I couldn't wait to get up out this bitch. These niggas in here were institutionalized forreal. I now had a full understanding of the documentary *13th* by Ava Duvernay.

I'd been down six months too long and couldn't for the life of me understand why this shit was being dragged out. The last time I'd spoken to Klein, he said I'd be out soon. Now knowing that Kaia had decided to go through with the pregnancy, I needed soon to change to yesterday real quick. How the hell didn't bro know she was pregnant? I knew he was around Kristen every chance he got, so unless Kaia made sure to duck him, there was no way he didn't know.

"Yo, you Maine?" A short, stocky dude with a fucked up fade approached me as I walked up the steps and made my way to my cell.

I ignored his question and kept it moving. Not taking my silence as a sign to go about his business, he followed. When he stepped into my cell, it was an instant sign of disrespect. Technically, this was my house, and he was trespassing.

"My nigga, you know how disrespect is handled around these parts. You sure you wanna take it there?" I asked, giving him a chance to rethink his decision.

"I'm saying though, no disrespect. I was just tryna see if you was dude from the mixtapes and shit. If so, I wanted to give you yo' props."

"Preciate that, but dig this, us being this close ain't the way to go about giving me my props. You could've said that shit in passing, dawg." He nodded in understanding and held out his hand for me to shake. "Boundaries, my nigga," I reiterated, nodding towards the cell door for him to exit.

"Respect, respect." I watched him walk out and my cellie walked in.

"Ju friend?" He questioned.

"Nope." Sitting down on my bunk, I stared straight at the wall.

Right now, my mind was on three things, getting the hell up outta jail, getting back to the music, and most importantly, getting my woman back. I didn't know how far along Kaia was, but I knew she needed me, and I didn't have too much pride to admit that I needed her, too. Besides, there was no breaking up, especially now that we had a child on the way. Kaia could be mad all she wanted, but thinking she was gon' skate on a nigga, she could hang that shit up.

~

"Brown, attorney visit," C.O. Banks called out to me the next morning.

I'd been sitting up in the same position since five this morning. I never slept too long in this joint. I didn't trust anyone, guards included. Standing, I didn't even think about freshening up. I'd seen how aggressive this C.O. got with the inmates, and with my temper, they would have to lock my black ass up for life if he jumped stupid.

The walk to the lawyer's visiting room was a short one. I could only hope that Klein had good news for the kidd. The room wasn't as bright as the family visitation room. The air was thick, stifling almost. The door opened and there Klein sat, waiting for me. He had a sly grin on his face, that shifted my mood instantly. I could sense the good news.

"Tell me something good, Klein." I opted out of sitting down and stood with my hands pressed against the table.

"I plan to Mr. Brown, and I really appreciate your patience. Like I mentioned on our previous visit, the precinct you were brought to when you were arrested is under investigation. The search of your brother's car proved to be an illegal search and I was able to get it thrown out." I nodded and waited for him to continue. Something in his smile suggested he had more to say. "Also, with help of a friend, I was able to get the dash cam from the officer's patrol car that night." He paused dramatically.

"I ain't gon' lie, Klein, you pissin' me off with all the pausing. Come on wit it, man." I probed, wanting him to get to the point.

"Alright, alright. The dash cam showed the officer, clear as day, planting the drugs in the trunk." Now it was my turn to smile. Standing up straight, I nodded and slapped him five.

"That's what the fuck I'm talkin' bout, Klein!" I swatted my fist in the air, knowing I was only moments away from being free again. "It took yo ass long enough. I don't want shit from out that cell, just tell them folks to process me."

"I'll be waiting for you out front."

It took another few hours to get me processed out. It could've taken all day for all I cared, as long as the end result was me on the other side of the steel doors. Once all the paperwork cleared, I was released. Klein was outside, posted, waiting for me in his E-Class Mercedes Benz, just like he said he'd be.

"Yo, where my brother?"

"He said he had something to take care of. Here's your phone."

I took it from him and went to my contacts to call Kaia first. I knew she wouldn't answer if my name showed on her caller ID, so I called private. It was ten in the morning, so I figured she was up. As the phone ring, I swiped my hand down my face, hoping she'd answer.

"Hello," her sleepy voice came through the phone, causing an instant smile to spread across my face.

"Wassup, shorty?"

"Who is this?" She responded, her voice now more alert than a few seconds prior.

"You don't know the father of your child's voice no more?"

"Nah, I don't understand fuck nigga." The click on the line let me know she had banged it on me.

While her feelings were warranted, the disrespect was not. I went to call her back and like I knew it would, the phone went straight to voicemail. I had to fix this shit by any means necessary. And the first thing we were gonna start with was clearing shit up about Kandice. Secondly, I was gonna kill the notion she had where she thought she was ever gonna address me as anything less than a man. Mad or not, disrespect would **not** be tolerated. I needed to get in touch with bro. I needed sound advice.

Ant

While Chloe sat across from me with her face turned up about my feelings for Kristen, I sat back, trying to muster up every ounce of patience I had left. Each second that passed without me knowing my girl's whereabouts was fucking my head up. And the fact that Chloe was tight- lipped about what I was sure she knew wasn't making the situation any better. Wherever she had lost her mind at, I needed her to find that motherfucka quickly. I was mere seconds away from forgetting she was Bre's mother and getting on good bullshit. I went to tell her just that, but my ringing phone stopped me.

Giving it a quick glance, I ignored the call, seeing it was Maine calling. I knew he was being released today but a celebration was the furthest thing from my mind at this point. With Kristen missing, I had tunnel vision. Knowing that Kane had orchestrated this shit infuriated me. I was prepared to tear the city up to find my woman.

"What's the address?" I turned my attention back to Chloe, who looked like she'd rather be anywhere but in my presence right now. "Yooo, I know you hear me talking to you."

"Wow, you didn't bat a fucking eyelash when I mentioned getting my ass beat, but you wanna run to her rescue? Fuck you, Antwon!" She spat, in disgust. She reached for the handle to get out, and the sound of me cocking my gun stopped her in her tracks.

"That nigga beaten yo ass ain't nothing compared to the pain I can inflict on you, trust me on that. I warned you about that nigga, but as usual, you wanted to find out the hard way. Well, a hard head makes a soft ass. Now, you gon' stop wasting my fuckin' time and give me the info!" My voice boomed through the car, making her jump. I wasn't playing and she needed to understand that before I broke my foot off in her ass. Just so she knew how serious this shit was, I placed my gun in my lap and kept my eyes trained on her face.

"You can't go after her or Bre's dead. He made that clear when I left, Antwon. I'm sorry but my daughter's life is worth much more than your girlfriend's." She couldn't even face me when that shit left her mouth. Before she or I knew what was happening, I'd hemmed her up by her shirt and yanked her towards me. "Antwon!" She exclaimed with wide eyes.

"He threatened my seed and you just now telling me?! You a simple motherfucka, you know that. Take me to him before I forget what my mama taught me and beat the fuck outta you. I'm not fuckin' playin', Chloe." She sniffled while rattling off the address.

Her spiteful ass had just signed her fate in my book. Shoving her back in the seat, I shifted my Camaro in drive, burning rubber as I sped off. My phone rang again, this time it was Kaia calling. My first mind was to ignore the call, but then again, I didn't want to look suspect.

"Hey, Ant?"

"Yea sis, wassup?"

"You seen my sister? I've been trying to call her, but her phone keeps going straight to voicemail." She didn't sound too worried, more annoyed than anything. If Kris was going to answer anyone's calls it would be her sister's.

"Nah, I tried calling her this morning, too, and no answer. I'ma bout to swing through her way now and scoop her." I wasn't telling a whole lie. I was about to scoop her, just not from home.

"Oh okay, well tell her to call me asap. I need to speak with her."

"You good? Have you spoken to bro? He was released this morning."

"No offense, but fuck yo brother," she snapped. "Have my sister call me please."

The call disconnected and I shook my head. That had taken an unexpected turn and though I wanted to inquire further, I wasn't in the headspace to go there. Leaving that situation alone, I focused on the one in front of me.

We'd driven about forty-five minutes before pulling up to the location Chloe said Kristen was being held. "Right over there, the house on the corner," she pointed out as I pulled into a small development. Taking note, I parked across the street.

"Let's go," I motioned to her as I got out. The look on her face let me know she wanted to challenge my direction but thought better of it. "You're gonna knock on the door and tell him that you came back because Bre is still with me."

"What if he's not here?"

"That's even better. I can just go in and get her."

"What about China?"

"Who the hell is China?"

"His woman, remember."

I had forgotten all about the other woman she'd mentioned as I had her replaying everything to me again during the drive. This dummy was even okay with sharing him with someone else. I shook my head at her poor decision making.

"That's a small thing to a giant, just knock, and I'll do the rest when whoever comes to the door." Taking in my surroundings as we walked side by side, I inhaled deeply and exhaled. All that went through my mind was the hell that may have been going on behind the closed doors of the townhome we now stood in front of. I was doing my best not to think about the state I might find my baby in.

I watched as Chloe put her hand up and knocked on the door lightly. I gave her a hard look that said, stop fucking around, and she knocked again, this time with urgency. I stood out of eyesight to her left. Hearing shuffling on the other side of the door and a baby crying, I became alert. *This nigga was holding my girl in the same house with a baby, sick ass individual,* I thought to myself. The person on the other side spoke through the door, inquiring who was there. Once Chloe announced herself, the woman quickly denied her entry, stating that Kane wasn't there.

"Let me in China. I gotta pee, girl," Chloe pressed.

She looked at me for confirmation and I nodded, letting her know the excuse sounded good to me. As soon as the door opened, I pushed my way into the house. Ol' girl looked like she wanted to scream, but my hand over her mouth stopped her before she could. She teared up when I put my gun to her temple. Hearing a baby's cries again, I glanced over her shoulder and saw the bassinet. Motioning for Chloe to grab the child, China shook her head wildly.

She knew without a doubt that shit had just got real.

Doing as I silently instructed, Chloe walked back over with the most beautiful, chunky, grey eyed baby girl. She was trying her best to fight her sleep, but her efforts seemed futile as she rubbed her eyes with her little chubby hands.

"Please don't hurt my baby."

I could see the love she had for the little girl, and I planned to use that to my advantage. Gesturing for Chloe to pass the baby to me, I cradled her in one hand while keeping my gun trained on China with the other.

"Where's Kristen?" The question was a simple one, but the look on her face showed that she was debating on whether she should answer. Without thinking twice, I turned the gun towards the baby. I hated to do it, but drastic times caused for drastic measures. Of course, I'd never hurt a child, but she didn't know that. She also didn't know that the safety was still on. "I'm not gonna ask you again, shorty."

"Down the hall, in the room to your right," she spoke quickly, reaching for the baby. I moved out of her reach and pointed the gun back at her. "Please, just get her and leave before he comes back. Don't hurt my baby."

"Back up and take me to the room. Chloe, follow behind her." Chloe fell in line and for some reason, each step towards the room my heart got heavier. I didn't know what to expect, but the feeling I had in the pit of my stomach told me it wasn't good. Once I got Kris out of here, I planned to never let her out my sight again until I caught up with this nigga Kane.

"You just a weak ass bitch, ain't you? They say jump, you say how high," China talked shit, taunting Chloe. Neither of us expected for Chloe to cock back and punch her in the back of the head, making her stumble forward. China recovered after a few seconds and went to charge Chloe, but my gun stopped her.

"Aye, aye, enough with that shit before I shoot both of y'all. Open the door, shorty, so I can get the fuck outta here. Unless you forgot I'm still holding yo baby, you may wanna cooperate."

It seemed like after Kris, Kane's goal was to recruit the dumbest hoes, Chloe included. I watched as she pulled a key from her pocket and unlocked the door. The room was dark as hell. From the light that came in from the hallway, I could tell the windows had been covered. The room was void of any furniture other than a twin sized bed that sat in the corner. I picked up on the distinct smell of dried blood in the air, which made the hairs on my neck stand up.

Passing the baby off to Chloe, I snatched China by her neck and pressed the gun to the back of her head, guiding her inside. I didn't see Kris on the bed, so I went around the other side of it. A somber look replaced the scowl I had on my face seconds ago when I noticed Kris in a fetal position, off in the corner. She wasn't moving from what I could see. I felt my grip on China's neck tighten, expressing my intense anger. She started to scratch at my hand, making me loosen my grip before pushing her aside to get to my baby.

Kris had on a white t-shirt that looked like it belonged to a man that stopped above her waist. On her bottom was a pair of green panties that appeared to have blood stains on them. I bit my lip so hard, I tasted blood. Going with my first thought, I checked her pulse. My baby wasn't dead, leading me to believe that she was just in shock. Pulling off my hoodie, I pulled her up gently and placed it over her head. It didn't cover her whole body, but it would do until we got to the car where I had the heat on. Picking her up, I stepped towards the door and looked at China who stood in the corner rubbing her neck.

"Tell Kane I'm on his ass, mark my words. And you better kiss that baby goodnight every night for the rest of your sorry ass days, bitch. It's because of her that I'm letting you live." I wanted nothing more than to pop her ass, but I had a heart. Moving swiftly, I made it outside and placed Kris gently in the back seat. "I'ma make this shit right, baby. I promise."

"Where we going?" Chloe asked with her hand on the handle of the passenger side door.

"You must be sick in the head if you think I'm letting yo ass in my car. You knew what was going on this whole fuckin' time and you ain't do shit to stop it! Got me over here interrogating you and shit, and my girl clinging to life! Fuck outta here before I run ya stupid ass over. Move Chloe!" She jumped back just as I put the car in drive and made good on my threat.

Using the hands-free option on my phone, I called my

private doctor and instructed her to meet me at my house asap. My mind drifted off, thinking about what it would take for Kris to recover mentally from whatever trauma occurred in that room. The physical scars would heal, it was the mental shit that stayed with you. Glancing up in the rearview mirror, I expected her to still be out of it, but she was wide awake. Her eyes bore into mine with a stare so intense, I wanted to look away.

Where there was once brightness, was now replaced with a sadness that I couldn't take. A piece of me broke for her as tears fell from her eyes with no audible sound. I never wanted to be privy to what took place in that room the few hours she was gone. She was crying out for me, and I needed to hold her. Not willing to wait until we got to my house, I pulled over on the side of the road. Hopping out, I went to the back seat and swung the door open. She didn't move when I picked her up and sat her on my lap. I didn't care that her panties were stuck to her or that her body smelled soiled; she needed me. My woman needed me now more than ever.

"Kristen, whatever thoughts may be going through your head right now, I want you to know that none of this shit is your fault, ma. I'm here for however long you need me to be. I won't ask any questions and we don't have to ever speak of what happened back there."

"Please, just take me home, Antwon." Her tone held an emptiness. I knew right then and there that her road to recovery wasn't going to be an easy one.

Kaia

After hanging up with Ant, I plopped back down on my bed and cast my eyes up to the ceiling. Annoyed that I couldn't get in touch with my sister was an understatement. It was rare that Kristen didn't answer when I called, and if for any reason she couldn't, she would send a text. I'd received neither. I planned to pay her a visit if she didn't hit me back in the next few hours.

I needed to vent in the worst way, and though I could talk to my girls about it, I needed my sister. Not only were my emotions all over the place due to the pregnancy but the bullshit with Maine had put them in overdrive. Hearing his voice on the phone and knowing he was home made me want to breakdown and cry, but I held firm. As far as I was concerned it was fuck him until our baby arrived. Once he or she made their debut, I would have no choice but to deal with him.

Seeing him sitting across from Kandice at the jail had me feeling dumb as hell. This was the same dude that made it known that he didn't want me coming to see him, but there he was on a fucking family visit with my opp. I couldn't give him the satisfaction of seeing me shed any tears, but when I got to Shanice's car, I bawled like a two-year-old. How could he play me like that? Kandice's presence only confirmed that the baby was in fact his. It was nothing we needed to discuss. By the time I got home, my tears had dried up and now I was pissed the fuck off and hungry.

I didn't want to be a step mommy. Hell, I had to figure out how I was gonna be a mama to my own child. Maine had put me in a real fucked up situation, and though it was unintentional, and the child was conceived before me, the situation was still fucked up. Just as I went to think another negative thought, the baby kicked me in my side.

"Ay, whose side are you on?" I spoke to my belly while rubbing my side. I smiled at the thought of the life growing inside of me. Out of all the people that were better prepared and maybe even more qualified than me, God had blessed my womb with this child.

"Hey, Kaia," my mother called out to me on the other side of my room door.

"You can come in, ma." I sat up with my back against the headboard. She entered, dressed in her scrubs for work.

"Hey, big mama. How you feeling?"

"I'm doing alright, about to get up in a few and head over to Kris's."

"Okay. You never said anything about the visit yesterday. How'd everything go?" The last thing I wanted was to give my mom something to worry about when it came down to my relationship with Maine, so I gave a simple answer.

"It was okay." I shrugged my shoulders. "He was released this morning."

"Oh, that's great!" Her face lit up while mine remained straight. She picked up on it, immediately. "Well shoot, don't be so excited, Kaia." I forced the smile that she was looking for and she frowned. "You might as well go head and spill it because if I have to ask, you know there will be no end to my questions."

"When I got there, he was on a visit already with his other baby mama," I spat, rolling my eyes.

"Say what now?" Her face turned up.

"Yea, Kandice, the girl from school." She nodded her head in recognition. "She's claiming that she has a baby by him. Ma, you should've seen the way they were at the visit. Like a little happy family. She had the baby there and everything. It's cool though, I'ma hold my baby down. I don't need Tremaine." I spoke out of anger, knowing I didn't really feel that way.

"See, what you not gon' do is become one of *those* girls." I looked at her with questioning eyes. "No child of mine will be a bitter baby mama. I raised queens and we ain't rockin' like that. What he has outside of the baby you two are about to have together has nothing to do with you. That is unless you want to remain in a relationship. Now, that is totally up to you. How do you know that the baby is his?"

"I don't, ma, but the thought that it could be is enough for me. It's a wrap for what I thought we had. And you're right, I'm not gonna be a bitter baby mama. I'm hurt, but I want him to be apart of our child's life." My head was all over the place because low key, I wanted him to be apart of mine, too. The fact that my dream of a little family had already ended before it could start tore me up on the inside.

"I hear you, but I think you should wait until you know for sure before you do anything drastic. In other news, I have a confession." She stood with a nervous smile. I sat up in the bed, holding my belly, anticipating her news. "Kaia don't be so damn dramatic," she said, making me laugh.

"What? I don't know what you bout to say. I wanna be prepared."

"Babeee, come here," she called out to my dad. He walked in, carrying a big teddy bear that looked half his size. Confusion was still plastered on my face, but I said nothing. "Soooo, at your last appointment, you told Dr. Ross you didn't want to know the sex of the baby yet. Well, I couldn't wait, so I had her email me the results and on this teddy bear, there's a bracelet with charms that spell out the baby's sex. Now, if I did too much and you really don't wanna know, we can wait…I guess."

I could only laugh at my mother with her sneaky self. Initially, I wanted to wait until Maine came home to find out the sex of our baby together, but since I wasn't fucking with him, there was no need to prolong the news. Motioning for my dad to bring me the teddy bear, I admired their creativity. Setting the bear down on my bed, I went straight for the bracelet. Reading the letters, my hand went up to my mouth to stifle my scream. The charms on the rose gold Pandora bracelet spelled *girl*.

"I know, right!" My mother exclaimed, wrapping her arms around me.

"Another girl for me to spoil," my dad commented with a nod.

I guess all that talking I did to the baby actually paid off. I got exactly what I wanted. A knock on the door made us pause our celebration. Hoping it was Kris so I could share the good news, I went to answer it myself. Unlocking and pulling it open without asking who it was, when I did identify the person, I quickly tried to close it.

"Don't do that, Kaia. Come on… let me talk to you, shorty," Maine pleaded, with his foot in the door to prevent it from closing.

"We don't have nothing to talk about and you better not push this door before you hurt my daughter." I was so focused on trying to stop him from entering, I had a slip of the tongue and blurted out the good news.

"Kaia, let the man in and stop acting crazy," my dad let out, walking over, and moving me to the side, allowing Maine to walk in. "Welcome home, kidd."

I looked on in disbelief as my parents embraced him. My mom took the cake, acting like I didn't just tell her about his other baby. With my face twisted and arms crossed tightly, resting on my belly, I stood off to the side, annoyed. His charming ass ate the attention up, expressing how happy he was that I decided to keep the baby and that he was gonna do right by us.

"Well, it was nice to see you again Maine, we gotta get going. Can I trust you to be here with her alone?" Maine nodded *yes* while I shook my head, *no.*

"Hell, Diane, she already pregnant, what else could they possibly do?" My dad pointed out, and Maine laughed. They both kissed my cheeks and made their way out the door.

"Your parents are a trip," Maine said, still laughing. I ignored him and made my way to the kitchen to find something to eat. Just because they let him in didn't mean I had to speak. "So, you really not gon' talk to me?"

He came up behind me as I looked in the fridge. I could feel his dick in between my butt cheeks. The satin pajama shorts I had on did nothing to create a barrier between us. Sticking to my guns, I continued to ignore him, while grabbing two eggs and bell pepper to make myself a quick omelet.

Creating a safe distance between us, I called out for my Alexa to play my chill out playlist. Imagine how fucked up Alexa had me when it played his song, "The One". My head fell back in total disbelief. I could hear him rapping along with the song and I fought myself not to turn around in fear that I'd forgive and forget the last twenty-four hours. I busied myself prepping my omelet to keep from jumping into his arms. The song went off finally and he wrapped his arms around me from behind. I felt myself losing control and basking in the fact that he was home.

He kissed my ear and I melted. "I missed you, Kaia. I missed you so much, baby. I love you, and even though she's not here yet, I love our baby girl, too. It's just us." Quickly remembering that Kandice was now apart of this "us" thing, I pushed him off me and resumed cooking. "You been having cravings and shit?"

"Did you ask Kandice the same question when y'all were communicating from jail?" I threw the question out there, fishing to see if he'd been in contact with her more than the one time that I was aware of.

"Stop playin' wit me. I didn't speak to that girl or see her while I was locked up. Yesterday was the first time and she just popped up. And why would I ask her that shit? She ain't my woman, *you* are."

"**Was**, I **was** your woman," I corrected him and took a bite of my food. He sat and watched me eat in silence. I was okay with that because I didn't have anything else to say regarding me being his *woman.*

"Man, we having a little princess." At the mention of the baby's sex, I felt her kick. It was like she was confirming what he said was true. "I'm happy as fuck." His smile was genuine and made me heart flutter.

"Yep, a little mini me." Grinning, I took another bite of my food.

"May I?" He asked before coming close to me again. I nodded and allowed him to rub my stomach. She started going crazy at his touch, making me jealous. She moved all the time but never this much for me. "She knows her daddy." He bent down to kiss my belly and when he came back up, his eyes met mine. I looked everywhere but at his face. "Look at me, shorty."

"I don't wanna make this harder than it has to be, Tremaine. As of now, we are co-parents. Nothing more, nothing less." At least that was what my mind was telling me to say, my heart said otherwise. I could tell he wasn't accepting of my decision, but he couldn't make me be with him.

"Nah, I'm not going for that. You don't get to make those decisions. And I know you only saying that shit based on what you think is going on with me and Kandice. If it makes you feel any better, I already had my lawyer swab me and he'll be reaching out to her to do the same with the baby. That way we can get all this shit straightened out."

It felt good to know that he was so adamant about taking the test, but I didn't want to take any chances on me being more hurt than I already was. So, if the results didn't work in my favor, at least we wouldn't be together.

"Okay."

He stayed until I finished my food and cleaned up behind me. Getting up, I let him know that I needed to get ready so that I could stop by Kris's house. He offered to take me, and I politely declined. I couldn't stand another moment of being in close quarters with him. He looked defeated, but there was nothing I could do about it. These were the cards we were dealt. I walked him to the door and when he leaned in for a kiss, I gave him my cheek.

Before he walked out, I asked the question that had been burning in my head. "What did she end up having?"

He turned around and sighed before answering, "A boy." Tears burned my eyes and I swallowed hard. In my head, I'd slammed the door closed, but I was stuck, holding it open as we stared at each other. "Don't cry, baby." Stepping back towards me, he cupped my face in his hands and placed a soft kiss on my lips. "Please don't cry."

I said nothing as hot tears cascaded down my cheeks. My heart was hurting. With no further words, he pushed me back slightly, reentering the house and closing the door behind him. With his hands on my stomach, he leaned in to kiss me again. This kiss had more hunger in it than the previous one, making my middle moist. Outside of pregnancy cravings, my emotions being on a level ten, and sleeping most of the day, I was always horny. And even with this being a sad moment, his touch heightened my senses, causing a tingling sensation to travel through my body.

Deepening the kiss, I wrapped my arms around his neck. In one swoop, he lifted me off my feet. I'd gained a couple pounds in the last few months, making me hippier, but he'd picked me up effortlessly.

Pulling my lips from his, I spoke what was on my heart. "I just want to be present in this moment, Tremaine. I need this moment. Make love to me right now and we can move accordingly going forward."

"There's no moving accordingly with me if it means that there's no us, Kaia. I'm gonna put this dick in you and make myself at home again. I've never given my heart to a woman, but I gave it to you, shorty. At the same time, understand that you don't get to put a nigga up on a shelf when shit get rocky. You mine and now that you have a part of me growing inside of me, it'll always be us. I love you." He used his mouth to tug at my bottom lip and lightly sucked on it. "I love you so much."

"I love you, too, Tremaine," I whispered into his mouth. Guiding me to my room, he gently placed me on the bed. "Make sure you lock the door," I instructed, hoping that my dad didn't return home and catch us in the act.

Yes, we all knew I was very pregnant and there was no secret how the baby was conceived, but the thought of me being caught face down, ass up was one I would never be able to explain. Closing and locking the door, Maine made his way back over to me, pulling his hoodie over his head and tossing it aside, along with his shirt. I leaned back on the bed, resting on my arms, taking him in. It was clear that he had been lifting weights by the fourth ab that was making its way through. He was fit prior to going away, but the difference now was noticeable.

Running his hand up and down my thighs, he tugged at my pajama shorts before pulling them off. The lace panties I wore were so soaked in my wetness. I could smell my essence as he spread my thighs. Sitting up straight, I lifted my shirt of over my head and unsnapped my bra, allowing my full double D cup breasts to be put on full display. I'd gone up a size and by the way he licked his lips and nodded, I could tell that he appreciated their fullness. Once we were both naked, he spread my legs and placed himself at my opening.

Although I would've loved a little four play, I was glad that he understood that we were about to have sex in my parents' home and time wasn't on our side to indulge the way we would have liked. Leaning down to kiss my lips, he slid into me slowly. It had been six months since I'd felt such pleasure, and I savored the moment as he gave me every inch.

"Ughhhh, ssssss," I hissed in pure delight. "Go slow,

please. Mmmmm, slow." I couldn't say when we'd be able to experience the moment again, so I wanted him to take his time.

"Shit, I missed this so much, Kaia. The feeling of you wrapped around me is something I can't even describe, shorty." Pumping in and out of me at a rhythmic pace, he reached for my right breast and twirled his tongue around my nipple. My mouth fell into an O and my pussy clenched around his shaft.

"Ahhhh, yessss, yesss, right there." Grinding his hips into me, he was careful not to put too much pressure on my protruding belly.

"Damn, she so wet for me, Kaia. You missed me too, huh." He spoke in between strokes.

"Yessss," I shamefully admitted. "I missed you so much. Ooouuu, you gon' make me cum."

He turned his speed up a little but didn't lose his rhythm. "Go head, baby, get yours. Gimmie dat cream." His voice sent me over the edge, and I let go, shaking beneath him.

"Ughhh, fuck!"

"Mmhmm, I feel you, baby. Keep it cummin'." My wetness dripped down my leg as he pulled out of me, still stiff, and turned me onto my side.

With his hand around my belly, he slid back into me and sunk his teeth into my neck. It felt so good, I could've sworn I saw stars. As he continued to thrust in and out, working my middle, I could hear his moans become more pronounced. It wasn't long before I was cummin' again and he was right behind me, filling me up with his seeds. Spent, we lay in silence, with him still inside of me, his dick twitching every now and then.

"Kaia, I...."

"Don't say anything. Can you just...go." It pained me to say the words, but I was doing what I felt was best.

Sighing, he kissed the back of my neck twice and pulled out of me. Getting up, I watched him grab his clothes from the floor and walk into my bathroom. He stood at the door for a moment to lock eyes with me. Not wanting him to see the tears that threatened to fall, I turned my head. Hearing the door close, I cried silently. A few moments later, he returned, and I felt my legs being opened, followed by a warm feeling between them. He was wiping the cum residue from my thighs and coochie lips. Setting the rag down on my nightstand, he wiped the tears from my eyes.

Placing his hand on my belly, he made a declaration. "I love you, Kaia. We gon' be good, I promise." I said nothing in response because I didn't know if we would be. "If you need me, I'm one call away."

With no further words, he made his exit. My heart ached bad, but I knew I had to keep it pushing. I couldn't afford to be sitting around depressed. So, although I wanted to shut myself off from the world, I got up from my bed a few minutes after his departure. Picking my head up, I continued with my plan, which was to head to Kris's house to see why she hadn't answered my calls. Getting dressed in a pair of Nike tights and matching shirt, I threw on my Nike hoodie, grabbed my wristlet and phone, and headed for the front door.

As I made my way to my car, I went to call her again, and this time the call connected.

"Where the hell you been?" I chastised off the rip.

"Sis, it's me, Ant. I need you to get to my house asap. I'ma text you the address. The key will be under the mat for you to let yourself in." The urgency in his voice put me on high alert. He didn't have to say anything else, I put the pedal to the metal before the text even came through. Something was wrong; I could feel it.

Kristen

I had been sitting in Ant's guest bedroom, staring at the wall for the last hour. Kane had truly done a number on me, and though I wanted this whole thing to be a nightmare that I could wake up from, it was very much my reality. My brain had yet to compute how far he was willing to go to get next to me. I knew he was crazy, but the last twenty-four hours that he'd held me hostage had proved that he was sick as fuck, too. At first, he would come in and profess his undying love for me, seeking the same in return, but I dared not to utter any words.

When that didn't work, he took off his nice guy mask and turned into the bastard I knew and used me as a human punching bag, hitting me with body shots only. Still, I remained adamant in my silence. I even did my best to hold onto my tears for as long as I could. That further enraged him to the point of no return, and he did the unthinkable. Shutting my eyes tightly, I fought not to relive the moment. I could hear the doctor that Ant had to come check on me outside talking to him about my condition.

"What you mean she won't let you touch her, Doc?"

"She's in shock, Antwon. When I go to touch her, she jumps. She also has a faraway look in her eyes that I'm sure you picked up on. The signs are consistent with someone that has been violated in the worse way."

"Wait, whoa, what you saying?"

Her response was low, so I wasn't sure what she may have revealed. Seconds later, the door opened slowly, and they both entered. "Baby, I need you to let her check you out, ma." He reached out his hands to touch mine and I allowed him to. "I just wanna make sure you straight."

"Did she..." I went to ask about what the doctor told him and his jaw twitched.

"Don't worry about that, bae. Just let the doctor do a quick checkup."

"I think it'd be best if I came back at another time. I can tell you've been through a traumatic experience, Kristen, and you need a minute. Give me a call in a few days, Antwon." The doctor gave me an empathetic look before turning to leave.

"Oh, my bad, excuse me." Hearing Kaia's voice, my eyes darted to the door. "What the fuck?! Why you look like that? What the fuck happened to my sister?" She sidestepped the doctor and tried to rush Ant, belly and all.

"Yo sis, chill before you hurt the baby." He stopped her and she snapped back. Thank God I was a little more cleaned up now because had she seen me earlier, she would've really flipped. "I'ma give y'all some time. Let me go talk to Doc." He kissed my forehead before walking the doctor out.

Kaia sat next to me with sad eyes. I could tell she wanted to cry but held it in. As if she knew I needed it, she hugged me tightly and I let out a muffled scream. Careful not to hurt the baby, I held onto my sister for dear life. The roles had been reversed in the moment, with her becoming the big sister, rubbing my back in a circular motion, allowing me to weep.

"He raped me, Kaia. Kane raped me," I finally admitted just above a whisper. The words had a sour taste to them as I spoke. She pushed me back a little and her hand went to her mouth.

"Wha... he... he did what? Kristen, nooo. I'ma kill that bastard!" She hugged me again and expressed how sorry she was, just as Ant had done earlier. I went on to explain to her how he snatched me up from the salon, along with China and Chloe. I didn't go into detail about the rape; it was too awful to relive. "Did you let the doctor check you out?" I shook my head *no*. I didn't want to be touched. "You have to, Kris. I'll stay and hold your hand. We gotta make sure his punk ass didn't give you nothing." I gave in and she called out to Ant. He re-entered the room within seconds. "Hey, is the doctor still here? She agreed to get checked out."

"Yeah. I wasn't letting her leave anyway. Let me go get her."

My heart smiled at the urgency and patience Ant had since finding me. To know that he was adamant on me being checked out thoroughly further proved how he felt about me. The doctor returned with a warm smile that reminded me of my mom. It was comforting and I was glad she didn't push the issue at first when I wouldn't let her touch me.

"You ready, sweetie?" She questioned, again ensuring my comfort. I nodded in response. "Okay. Antwon, I need you to step out and I'll call you back once we're done."

He looked to me for confirmation, and I gave him a light smile. Walking over to the bed, he kissed my forehead and headed back out. Once the door closed, the doctor got to work. Kaia held my hand as she used the same equipment that I recognized from my yearly pap smears with my gynecologist. I tensed up when she spread my lips to swab my vagina. Flashes of the ordeal went through my head, making my eyes water. The doctor paused and looked up at me.

"I got you, sis," Kaia whispered in my ear while squeezing my hand. She gave the doctor a head nod to continue. The whole checkup took another twenty minutes to complete. As she went through the process, she let me know what she was sending tests out for.

"Alright love, we're all set. I am seeing a lot of vaginal tearing here and inflammation. Without you telling me, I already have an idea of what happened. Right now, the goal is to ensure that we get you cleared of any diseases. Last thing I want you to do is pee in this cup for me so we can do a quick pregnancy test." I shot up on the bed when she mentioned pregnancy.

"No need, ain't nobody pregnant." The fact that she would even insinuate such a thing made my blood boil. The thought of being pregnant with Kane's demon seed made my hands clammy.

"You sure you don't wanna take a test? I mean just to rule it out?" Kaia inquired with uncertainty.

"Positive. You think I can get those results rushed, Doc pop?"

"I'm taking them to the lab soon as I leave here. You take care of yourself, Kristen." I thanked her and watched as she packed up her things before leaving.

After all that poking and prodding, I needed another shower. Leaving Kaia sitting on the bed, I went to do just that. Stepping into the steaming hot shower, I scrubbed my body for the second time, hoping to wash Kane's scent off me. I'm sure no one else could smell it, but it was still very much apparent to me. I closed my eyes to block out the images that kept flashing in my head. A knock on the door made me open them.

"Babe, it's me," Ant announced himself.

"I'll be out in a minute!" I snapped before sliding down the wall in the shower with my hands covering my face.

I couldn't be this girl. I didn't want to be a victim. And I damn sure didn't want my family treating me like some fragile piece of glass. Oh God, speaking of family, how was I gonna tell my parents? I stayed in the shower another twenty minutes before finally stepping out. Standing in front of the full-length mirror, naked, I examined myself. From underneath my breasts to the mid part of my thigh I had bruises. All courtesy of Kane and some from China when she could get her licks in. There were even hickies all over my breasts.

"Kris, we should call, mo..." Kaia's voice trailed off and I attempted to grab my towel to cover myself but was too slow. "Anttttt!" She yelled out for Antwon just as I wrapped the towel around me.

"Noooo, Kaia, don't do that!" He had only seen the bruising on my thighs due to me wanting to be alone when I showered. I knew that seeing the hickies would turn him off and the additional bruising would take him over the edge.

"Fuck that, Kristen, he need to see this shit. It'll give him more incentive to find Kane's ass and I hope he tortures him when he does. Look at your body, what the fuck!" She pulled at my towel, but I held it tightly, swatting her hand away.

"Ouchhh, stoppp." Kaia was so hell bent on ratting me

out to Antwon, she didn't take into account that the bruises were fresh.

"What's going on?" Ant stood at the bathroom door, his face twisted in confusion.

"Show him, Kris."

"Show me what?"

"The bruises. She has bruises all over Ant, look." She tried again to pull on the towel, but I held it tight.

Ant walked closer, putting his hand on the side of my face. The way he looked at me wasn't with a look of sympathy, it was a look that let me know I was safe with him. Closing my eyes again, I let the towel fall to the floor. The silence that filled the air made me nervous. Reopening my eyes, he was still standing in front of me with a blank look. Before I could say anything, he turned and walked away abruptly. I was damaged.

Kaia

I had been Kris's shadow for the last couple days and if I had to be up under her for the next couple months, I would. My mind was still reeling from what she'd revealed about what she endured at the hands of Kane. I swear if I wasn't big and pregnant, I would've handled him my damn self. One bullet to the dick and another to head. And I was far from a killer, but I'd turn into one behind my sister.

Every day, she was still giving me push back on taking the pregnancy test, leaving me to wonder if she actually was pregnant. It was the sole reason I continued to bring it up.

Ant had been in and out since seeing the bruises on Kris's body. More out than in though, day and night. I knew it was taking a toll on my sister, I also understood that Ant was out for blood. If I was being honest, I was scared for Kristen. She didn't talk much, and the vibrant person that was once there was gone. She refused to tell our parents what happened and had resulted in delivering messages through me to them. I wanted so bad to tell my mother what had gone down, but I couldn't betray Kris's trust.

I sat up from the bed in the guest bedroom and went to check on her. Grabbing my phone, I slipped on my fuzzy slippers and headed two rooms down to the master suite. From outside the door, I heard her and Ant in a heated exchanged. They argued respectfully so I was unable to hear them from the room I slept in.

"Why you can't just take the test?"

"Because I don't want to, Antwon. I'm not pregnant so why are we wasting our time?"

"Last I checked, yo ass wasn't a doctor. What's the worst thing that could happen if you took the test, ma?"

"I'm not taking it, end of story. Please respect that." Her voice was low, and I could tell she was agitated.

"Aight," Ant replied, sounding defeated. I went to knock but stopped when I felt an arm wrap around my waist. I didn't have to turn around to know it was Maine. His cologne gave him away.

"Why you out here being nosey?" He questioned while rubbing my belly, making the baby move.

"Ain't nobody being nosey and could you back up a little." I pushed him back with my butt. His hard on swiped my ass cheeks and I shivered a little thinking about the last time we'd made love.

"Why you don't want me close to you? Scared I'ma make that thang wet?"

"Boy please. What you doing over here anyway?" I waved him off, knowing his statement held nothing but truth.

"I wanted to check in on you and my baby. I bought you some food, too. It's downstairs in the kitchen." I wanted to smile at his attentiveness but didn't want to forget that I wasn't fucking with him. I expressed my thanks, though. "You don't have to thank me, it's my job to do stuff like this."

"You do stuff like this for your other baby mama, too?" I asked, sounding salty as hell.

"I'm not even gon' dignify that with an answer. You bout to blow me with that silly shit. Excuse me." He shook his head at me and went to knock on the door.

Annoyed that I had come off as jealous, I moved to the side, with my face screwed up. Maine announced himself and the door opened. Seconds later, Ant came out and closed the door behind him. I gave him a half hug and encouraged him to hang in there. I knew Kris was giving him the blues. He was very understanding, and I not only admired that, but I respected it.

"Aight with all the hugging shit." Maine pulled me back, putting space between me and Ant.

"Nigga, shut up. Thank you for that sis, you gon' be here a little while?"

"Yea, then I'ma head home to pick up some clothes. Oh shoot, I forgot I had an appointment today. Let me call Sha and Mecca and see if they still coming." I had been so wrapped up in making sure Kris was good, I forgot I was due for a checkup. I was entering my seventh month and becoming a worry wart.

"Oh, so I ain't shit, huh?" Maine shook his head, mugging me.

"Huh? What are you talking about? They always go to appointments with me." I didn't see the big deal, but after thinking about it, I could understand why he felt slighted.

"Well, I'm home now, so whenever you have an appointment, I should be privy to that info so that I can clear my schedule to be there," he said matter factly. "I'ma be waiting for you in the car. Ion know what you got going on, but you starting to piss me off. Bro, I'll be back in a few." He didn't give me a chance to protest before walking off. I sucked my teeth and stomped off, back in the direction of the guest room.

"Get used to it!" Ant yelled out. I gave him the finger and kept walking.

I don't know why he think he runnin' shit, I thought to myself while getting dressed. Since carrying around all this belly, leggings and oversized hoodies had become my thing. Today was no different. Throwing on a pair of Nike Pro leggings, a hoodie, and my leather jacket, I slid my feet into a pair of Uggs. Giving myself a quick fit check in the mirror, I grabbed my purse and headed back to Kris's room.

The door was now fully open, and I could see her laying in Ant's lap, watching tv while ran his fingers through her hair, massaging her scalp. He knew how to soothe her.

"Hey sis, I have an appointment for the baby, but I won't be gone too long." She sat up to respond to me.

"Oooh, I wanna go." She surprised me. We had been trying to get her to go out and she had been shutting us down.

"Really? Okay, come on." This was a big step, so if I had to be late for my appointment to wait for her to get ready, so be it. "I'm gonna wait for you in the car. You know Maine is probably cursing me out with his impatient ass." I made my way downstairs and just as I expected, Maine had something to say about how long I took.

"You had a hard time getting dressed or something?"

"Shut up, I was waiting for Kris. She said she wanted to come. This will be her first time being out since the incident."

"Oh, aight, my bad."

"Exactly, talking all that ra-ra, and don't even know what's going on." My phone buzzed and it was a text from Kris telling me to go ahead and she'd meet me at the doctor's office. "She's gonna meet us there."

He gave me a head nod and we drove off. The whole drive there, he didn't talk to me, and I didn't bother sparking up a conversation. Even though I didn't want to talk to him, I did feel some type of way that he was now igging me. I was the only person who actually had a right to be in my feelings. Annoyed and on the verge of tears, I turned up the radio just as H.E.R's "Damage" crooned through the speakers.

If I let you, don't take me for granted, yeah. If I'm worth more than you could manage, manage, yeah. Open with me, oh, we could be honest. Closer to me, oh, givin' me solace. Promise that you won't let me fall. Holdin' me tight, lovin' me right, givin' me life. All night, you could be...

Sniffling, I turned to look out the window. I hated the state that we were currently in. I hated it bad.

THE DOCTOR'S appointment went well, with Dr. Ross reconfirming that were having a little girl. It was cute to see Maine's face light up when he saw our baby girl on the screen. I even let him hold my hand during the ultrasound. Kris decided not to come at the last minute, and I was okay with that. The fact that she made the attempt was more than enough for me. She'd taken a necessary step, which made me hopeful about her recovery.

"You have a name picked out for her yet?" Maine asked as we hopped on the highway.

"Yea, I wanna name her Kymani Amor. You have any names in mind?"

"Nah, I want whatever you want, shorty."

I smiled at his response. The charming shit was getting to me, and he was making it hard to stay mad. When the car finally stopped, we were in front of his building. He said nothing as he got out of the car and walked around to my side, opening the door for me.

"What we here for?" I stayed planted in the seat, ignoring the hand he held out.

"I wanted some time alone with you and I knew that wasn't possible at Ant's crib. I wanted to show you something, too." I was prepared to be stubborn, but I put my hand in his, knowing he wasn't taking no for an answer. In his apartment, I consciously looked around for any remnants of Kandice or her baby. It made my skin crawl thinking about the two of them being here, playing family. "No one's been here, so you can stop lookin' for shit," he said, reading my mind. "I need to cover your eyes so that you can see the surprise I'm working on."

Not giving me a chance to object, he stood behind me with his hands covering my face. Guiding me through the house, we stopped after a few steps, and he moved his hand. As my eyes surveyed the space, I got choked up looking at the beginning stages of a baby room for our little girl. Seeing that he'd only been home a few days and had found time to do this blew my mind. The room was all white with grey and pink accents. Fit for the little princess we were bringing into the world.

"Babeeeeee, I mean Maine," I quickly corrected myself. "This is so beautiful. When did you have time to do this?"

"After leaving your crib, I called up my cousin, and she hooked me up with an interior designer. If you want to change the colors, we can. I just told the lady to do some girly shit that she'd want for her own kid." He shrugged like it wasn't a big deal, but it was for me. The fact that he took the time to even think about doing this was pretty dope. "It's still in the beginning stages, but it's coming along."

"I don't wanna change anything, this is perfect. Daddy did a good job, mamas," I said to my belly. Walking into the room, I gave myself a quick tour, taking in the details. "You did good, Tremaine. Like, really, really good. I can't wait till' it's completed." A yawn escaped me, and I shook it off. "Whoo, I'm getting sleepy. I think I'm ready for my midday nap."

"You can just sleep here. You still have stuff in the closet." I gave him a look that said I'd rather not. "Come on, why drive all the way back to Ant's house when there's a comfortable ass bed in my room?" He made a good point, but I still wasn't sold.

"I don't want you to get the wrong idea."

"The wrong idea about what?" I gestured between the

two of us. "Man, go head and get in the bed, shorty. You already made it clear that you ain't fucking with me, cool. You can get some rest and when you get up, I'll take you back over to Ant's." He walked off, leaving me standing in the middle of the room, feeling like the bad guy.

CHAPTER 6

Maine

Being around Kaia and not being able to interact with her the way I had become used to was blowing me. Every few seconds she made it known that we weren't on that type of time. I thought that the surprise would be a step in the right direction, but once again she shut my ass down. Something had to give though, I didn't know how much longer I'd be able to be in this space with her.

"Hey, do you mind making me something to eat?" She asked from where she lay on the couch. She decided she didn't want to sleep in the bed, and I wasn't about to force her to.

"Yea, I mind, but I know my princess gotta eat, so I guess I have to." I was gonna give her the same kind of energy she was giving me, dry as fuck.

"You don't have to if you don't want to. I can just order from Uber Eats." Now she had an attitude.

I ignored her and went to the kitchen to heat up some leftover lasagna my mom had dropped off the night before. Entering the kitchen a few seconds later, she sat at the counter, twiddling her thumbs while I checked the messages on my phone. It was awkward as hell, but shit, it was what it was. The microwave dinged and I set my phone down to get her plate. Placing it in front of her with a fork and napkin, I retreated to the living room.

Kaia was bringing out a softer side of me that I didn't know existed. That shit was not cool because I was starting to feel like a sucka ass nigga. I felt like I was begging her, in not so many words to stay at my crib. What part of the game was that? Getting comfortable on the couch, I turned the tv on. Feeling the other side of the couch weighed down, I looked over to see she had come over with her food.

"This is good," she complimented with her mouth full. "I mean to ask you earlier, how's Rel and Kelsey been since going back home?"

"They straight. I've been checking in with them daily. Linda is going to her classes as promised and staying clean. They know that I'm still one phone call or text away."

"That's good. Give me a number for them so I can stay in

contact, too. Us not being together shouldn't affect the bond I've grown with them."

Ignoring her, I kept my eyes on the tv. The last part of her statement she could've kept. As the silence engulfed the air again, I could hear my phone ringing in the kitchen, making us both look in that direction. Not feeling like getting up, I glanced down at my Apple watch to see who was calling. Of course, Kandice would pick this very moment to ring my phone. Shaking my head, I answered so that Kaia would know I wasn't hiding anything.

"Yo," I answered dryly.

"Hey, baby daddy, did you get the test results yet?" I watched Kaia get up from the couch out the corner of my eye. I could hear her moving around the kitchen making noise, further letting me know she was pissed.

"Nah, I didn't. And I told you not to call my phone. If you need to reach me, go through my lawyer."

"No need for me to do that. I got the results in the mail today, they sittin' right in front of me. I thought we could open them together. That way you can be surprised, and I can confirm what I already know," she taunted.

"Well, nothing came through on my end yet."

"No problem, I'll read them to you. Tremaine Brown you are 99.9 percent the father of Chase Tremaine Brown. Congratulations!"

Everything stopped and a loud crash made me jump up from the couch and run to the kitchen. My eyes traveled from the shattered plate at Kaia's feet to the look of anguish on her face. All I could do was hang my head.

"Helloooo, did you hear me? You the daddy, just like I…"

I hit the end button on my watch before Kandice could continue bragging. Adding insult to injury, a text came through with a picture of the results that showed clear as day that I was indeed the father of her son.

"Kaia," I called out before walking towards her.

"You said the baby wasn't yours," she let out in a low voice while stepping backwards.

"I was confident that he wasn't. Baby, she trapped me, I swear. Come on, be careful before you cut your foot." Her eyes were honed in on me. The glass on the floor was the least of her worries.

"I can't do this with you, Maine. I thought of all the ways I could be accepting of you having a child outside of me, and with her… I just can't. Please, take me home." Her saying she couldn't hold it down was enough to break a real nigga.

"You treatin' me like I planned this shit. That stupid bitch trapped me and you telling me you not willing to stick by a nigga's side? What about how I feel?! So, what, you gon' stop me from seeing my daughter now?"

"I never said that, but you made the choice to lay down with her. So yes, this is your fucking fault!" She bucked at me.

"You know what, let me get this glass up and I'ma take

you home. I can't deal with this shit either." I did just that and dropped her off at her crib without any further words exchanged between us.

IT HAD BEEN a week since I found out that Chase was my son. Since then, Kandice had been blowing up my phone every day wanting or needing something. I was two seconds from getting my mama on her ass. I hadn't been in the studio in a while, so I was headed there to get some shit off my chest. Being in the studio was my therapy. Linking up with Playboy, he played me a couple new beats and I went in. By the time we were done, I had three tracks for him to mix.

"That's what I'm talking about, bruh," Ant spoke into the intercom from the other side.

"Yooo, what's good. When you get here?"

"Couple minutes ago, I needed to finish up some contracts. You was in that bitch zoned out. Come out and politic with me."

I sat the headphones down and followed him out of the studio and into the lounge. I had only spoken to Ant over the phone lately. He had a lot going on with Kris and I knew he needed his space. Even though I was going through my own shit, I made sure to keep my ear to the streets regarding any sighting of that pussy, Kane. We were on him like white on rice when we caught up to him. "You goin' in like you ready to go on tour or something my nigga."

"Shit, I am. Now that we've put the streets on the back burner, I'm ready to see what this rap money looking like, forreal." I wasn't hurting for no bread by any means, but you could never have too much. "Plus, with me having two mouths to feed now, a nigga gotta get out here and get it."

"I hear you, man. Have you seen the baby since finding out the test results?"

"Nah. To be honest, man, I ain't tryna be around Kandice. This crazy broad been on my line asking for shit like a car, bigger apartment, and a monthly allowance. This hoe ain't ask for no pampers, formula, baby clothes, or nothing for lil' man. She think she done hit the fucking jackpot with me." Just speaking Kandice's name pissed me off, imagine having to *actually* be in her presence.

"That's gonna be for the next eighteen years, bro. You gon' have to deal with that shit for the sake of your little one. Our pops was never around, you don't want that to be neither one of your kids' story. That's why it's so many damn serial killers out this bitch."

"Yea, I hear you. How's everything going with Kris?"

He sighed before answering. "We taking it day by day. I gotta get this nigga, bro. Every day I let my head hit the pillow and he's not in the ground, I feel like less than a man. How I let him get that close to take my girl?" He swiped his hand over his face and his jawline flexed. A motion we both did when we were frustrated.

"That shit ain't yo fault. And we gon' find him, believe that. Right now, he think he got the upper hand, but the streets is watching."

We chopped it up a little more about events he had planned for the other artists and how he planned on setting up a tour to get my name back out there. I needed to get that done asap. Kaia was due in another two and a half months, and I wasn't trying to miss the birth of my daughter for nothing or nobody.

"Aight, I'ma get up outta here. I gotta go check in on Kristen. Oh, and before I forget, you need to go check up on Kaia." My ears perked up at the mention of her name.

"What you mean, check up on her? Something wrong?"

"I mean she's pregnant with your baby, so check up on her. She might not be fucking with you, but she and the life she's carrying is still your responsibility." I nodded in agreement. I was tryna give her space, but he was right. I had to pull up on Kandice first, we had to get an understanding.

I sat outside in my car coaching myself so that I wouldn't get mad when Kandice said some stupid shit out her mouth. She still lived at home with her mom and even though I hadn't met her, I knew I wouldn't like her because she'd given life to Kandice. I was on some Avant shit, every time I saw her ass, I got a bad vibe. Making my way up the littered steps in her building, I knocked hard on her door like the sign taped on front suggested. I shook my head at the ghetto notice. The door opened a few seconds later and a heavy-set woman stood behind it with a sour look on her face.

"Who you looking for?"

"Is Kandice here?" I answered with just as much base as her.

"Yea, she here. Kandi!" She hollered before stepping aside to let me in. I could've been here to smoke Kandice and everybody in her crib, and she just let me in. I made a mental note to mention it. I had to know that my son was safe at all times. *At least the inside looks better than the outside,* I thought to myself as I walked in. "You can have a seat." The woman offered while pointing to the sectional.

"I'm good."

"What happened, ma? Oh, what you doing here?" Kandice came into the living room with the baby strapped to her.

"As much as you blow my phone up, you should be happy to see me. I came by to check in on the baby and see what **he** needed."

"Oh, this is the infamous Maine, huh? Well, we need a better car so we can get the baby around. You need to start giving up some child support too, so she can start paying some bills round here. Tell him, Kandice," her mother encouraged.

"She don't have to tell me a motherfuckin' thing. Again, I ask, what does the **baby** need?" They were wasting my time.

"Ma, can you go so I can talk to him alone?" I watched as her mother threw her hands up and left the room. The baby started to cry and stir in the contraption she was holding him in. "Here, hold him while I make a bottle."

Before I could say anything, she unsnapped the piece that held him in place and practically threw the baby to me. It was a good thing that I had a lot of practice with Bre when she was born. I held lil' man in the crook of my arm, as he stared at me, alert, like he was trying to figure me out.

"I'm your dad, lil' man," I whispered to him, and I could've sworn he smiled a little. It didn't take her long to come back with the bottle.

"Here you go, try feeding him." I accepted the bottle she handed to me, and he latched onto it soon as I put it up to his mouth.

"Why you not breast feeding? Ain't that like the best form of milk?"

"Yea, but he not tryna latch on and I don't want him to starve, so formula is the next best thing." I asked a series of other questions, taking mental note of her answers. Little did she know, I was filling her out to see how she'd been mothering my son. So far so good, I didn't see a reason to have my mama to pull up on her. "So, how ya girl feeling about us having a baby?" She stood in front of me with her arms folded and a smirk on her face.

"We not doing that. I'm here strictly about my son. We need to come up with a suitable schedule for me to see him.

Also, when I give you money for him, it should only go to things **he** needs, not shit for you or yo mama. And I want a receipt as well. You can look shocked and have an attitude all you want. This is what it is, or you can take me to court." I handed her the bottle Chase had finished and set him up on my shoulder to burp him.

"Whatever. Right now, he need a whole bunch of shit, so will you be able to take me to get it or provide a car for me to go?" Still, she was looking for ways to be around me or seen with me.

"Nah, you can Uber or drive the car I see in the driveway. Matta fact, send me the list of stuff and I'll pick it up and drop it off." After he burped, I handed him back to her just as he started to doze off. "I'ma hit you with a schedule and we can work things out from there." I left out feeling like I'd made some headway with one baby mama. Now I had to see if the other was even willing to talk to me.

Kristen

Me and the First Response pregnancy test had been in a stare off for the last thirty minutes. With Ant leaving out to handle business, it gave me time to weigh the pros and cons of taking the test. Both he and Kaia had been pressuring me about it and I had run out of reasons as to why I didn't need one. The truth was, I was scared to confirm what I already knew. Something in my heart told me Kane wasn't through with me yet, and to further fuck with my head, he had planted a baby inside my womb.

Ant had been so adamant about the test that he hadn't thought about the end result. Taking a deep breath, I opened the box, peed on the stick, and set an alarm on my phone. A pink and white stick was about to change the trajectory of my life. The two-minute wait felt like forever before the alarm went off, sealing my fate. I was indeed pregnant. My heart raced, my hands shook, and my face felt hot.

With the sudden urge to vomit, I rushed over to the toilet and hurled up the food I'd eaten earlier. Things couldn't get more fucked up than this. Pregnancy took the fucking cake. I threw up to the point where I began to dry heave. Cradling the toilet, I cried. I didn't see a way out of the darkness and that scared me the most.

"Bae, where you at?" Hearing Ant, I jumped up and slammed the bathroom door shut, locking it behind me.

"I'm in the bathroom," I responded, turning on the water in the sink to rinse my mouth. Throwing the pregnancy test back in the box, I tossed it in the trash. It wasn't the smartest move, but it would have to do for now.

"Wassup, ma?" He greeted me with a hug and kiss as I walked out into the room. "You aight?"

"I'm good," I responded before crawling back in the bed and pulling the covers over my head. I had the room set up just the way I felt—empty. All the curtains were drawn, leaving little light, and silence fell over me.

"Getcho ass up, now!" I heard a loud voice that I'd recognize anywhere. Peeking from under the covers, I watched Heaven barge into the bedroom and open the blinds. I moaned in aggravation, but deep down I knew it was what I needed. "Let's go… get it up, we not doing this. I can't believe I had to find out everything from Ant and I barely even like him."

"Forreal my nigga?" Ant interrupted, making me giggle.

"My bad, you know I fucks witchu boy."

"Come on cousin, get up. We bout to bring you back to life. You have a business to run and we not gon' let no bitch made nigga knock you off yo square. I gave you a week to come to me, now, here I am." She pulled the covers off me and pulled me up by my arms. "You can go now, I got this," she said to Ant who shook his head.

"How you gon' kick me out my own shit?" She put one hand on her hip and shooed him with the other. "Aight, Kris, I love you. I'll be downstairs if you need me."

"I love you, too, babe. Thank you." He winked and walked out.

"Okay, first thing first, let's do something with this hair, my girl." My hair had been in a messy ponytail for the last week. The only comb through I had was when Ant would run his fingers through it while I laid in his lap. "Where are your combs and stuff?"

"Top drawer, over there." I pointed and leaned back against the sink in the bathroom.

"Ahhhh, bitch you pregnant?!" Heaven exclaimed, snatching the First Response box out of the trash. She just didn't give a damn about my privacy. Holding the box up to my face, she shook it. The look must've conveyed that I didn't share the same excitement. "What did I miss? You not happy?"

"Would you be happy if there was more than a possibility that you were carrying your rapist' baby?" I asked with a straight face. "Before you think about answering that, don't. And please don't say you're sorry, I've heard enough of that this past week." She shook her head, and I allowed her to hug me. "I just want some sense of normalcy back, Heaven, so just...be my cousin right now."

"Okay, you got it. And as your cousin I need to be able to tell you the truth. Your hair really looks a damn mess. You can't be out here disrespecting the Phillips name like that, boo. Come sit down and let's get you back together." I chuckled at her shade.

This was what I needed to get my mind out of that dark place. Taking the box from her, I tossed it back in the trash and told her to remind me to take it out before Ant saw it. After a good wash and trim, my hair had been restored with its natural bounce. Now, I needed to do something about the bags under my eyes from lack of sleep. While cleaning up, Heaven caught me up on what was going on at the shop as we were still in the stages of reconstruction after the fire. We had about another month before we could open back up. I had to get my mind right before I could step foot back in there.

"Thank you for keeping everything together for me, boo. I owe you one."

"I'll take a paid two-week vacation for two hundred, Alex."

"And with that time off, find you a new place of employment, heffa." She laughed and gave me the finger.

"Whateva. Hey, is Kaia having a baby shower?"

That was a good question. I had been so caught up in my own shit, I didn't even think to ask her. Knowing my mom though, she probably already had something in the works.

"Not sure, let me call my mother and see." Grabbing my phone, I went to dial her number, and a call came in from a nine two nine area code. I didn't recognize the number but answered anyway.

"It's good to know you're still alive. I'll be seeing you soon, my love." The line went dead in my ear, and I felt myself shaking.

"Kris, you're shaking, you good?" Heaven touched my shoulder, but my body wouldn't stop trembling. "Okay cuz, take a deep breath. Come on, breathe it through." I did as she instructed and kept taking deep breaths until my body started to settle.

"He gotta die, Heaven. Kane has to die. That's the only way he'll leave me alone."

"Tell me what you need me to do."

While Kaia was my right hand, Heaven was my left. I didn't expect anything less than the response she gave. I told her the plan I'd been putting together in my head for the last week, down to the execution, and she was for it. I not only had something for Kane but China's ass as well. I couldn't do too much to Chloe, but a severe ass whooping was on the horizon.

THE NEXT DAY, I woke up to someone playing in my hair. I looked up to find Bre sitting up by my head, locked in on the tv.

"Well, hey little lady." She glanced down at me and smiled, showing her pearly whites.

"You up, Kris. You was sleepy, huh?" I laughed at her facial expression. She was a little old woman.

"Yea, I was. I missed you, little lady." I reached up to hug her and she giggled once I started to tickle her.

"I missed...you...too," she let out in between laughs. "Kris, you still like my daddy?" Confused by her line of questioning, I sat up and faced her.

"Why you ask that, mamas?"

"My daddy said you ain't feeling him." Her face was serious, and I did everything I could not to laugh.

"You know you're too much right." She smiled and shook her head. "To answer your question, I *am* feeling your daddy. I love him very much." She seemed satisfied with my answer and cuddled up under me, focusing back on the tv. No matter the ill feelings I had towards her mother, Bre was my little baby. She was so charismatic and truly one of a kind.

Her laying under me made me think about the child I was carrying. I hadn't told Ant about the pregnancy, and I didn't plan to. I couldn't see myself giving birth to a child spawn from Kane. How could I love the baby of my rapist? The door opened and Ant walked in, pulling me from my thoughts.

"I see Bre found a way to get in here and wake you up."

"Yea, but you know I don't mind. This my lil boo."

"Yea daddy, I'm her boo. She feelin' me, right Kris?" All she did was repeat what she heard, not knowing the meaning behind it. We both laughed and I confirmed with a head nod.

"That's wassup. Can you go lay on your little couch while I talk to Kris right quick?" She complied and he took her place in the bed.

"How you feeling?"

"Better. Thank you for inviting Heaven's crazy ass over to pull me out of my funk." I leaned in and placed a soft kiss on his lips.

"No problem, ma. I wanna ask you something." He held my hand, and I felt my underarms start to sweat. All of a sudden, I remembered that I didn't get rid of the pregnancy test I took yesterday. I kept a straight face so I wouldn't give away the fact that I was nervous. "Are you pregnant?" I wasn't sure if he noticed, but now my palms were starting to sweat. I wanted to deny that I was, but if he was asking, then he just needed confirmation for what he already knew.

"Yes," I admitted.

"Why didn't you tell me, ma?"

"Because I'm not keeping it," I said matter factly.

"And I have no say so?"

"Not if there's a chance that the baby is Kane's you don't. I don't wanna risk it." The look he gave me made me look away. I couldn't let his concern and doubt change my mind.

"You got that. I'ma take Bre out to the park for a little while."

"She's good, she can hang with me."

"Nah, you can make decisions with the little one you're carrying, I got her." His statement cut me deep and I felt a tightness in my chest. Not wanting Bre to see me cry, I held it together long enough to tell her I'd see her later. She pouted a little when I told her I wasn't going. A promise of ice cream from her dad and more ice cream when I saw her again cleared that right up.

Once they left, I packed a small bag and ordered an Uber. If Ant couldn't understand the why behind my decision to abort this pregnancy, then I didn't know what to tell him. It was my cue to go home, only I was afraid to be alone. Changing the Uber destination, I was en route to my parent's house for clarity.

Kane

Hearing the fear in Kristen's heavy breathing made my dick hard. I wanted her to know that even though she had gotten away from me physically, I still had her mentally. It was all a part of my plan. I knew I wouldn't be able to keep her long once Ant discovered she was missing. I wanted her to walk around looking over her shoulder, wondering when I'd strike again.

Not only did she cost me my job, but for her to allow Ant to embarrass me in front of a crowd was a no no. As soon as he found out I used to deal with Kristen he stopped my money supply. Good thing I always made sure to have a rainy-day fund. I had a shit load of tricks up my sleeve for him and his non-talent having ass brother. Hell, I may even find something for one of my old police buddies to pin on their crooked ass mother.

"Are you serious right now? You don't hear the baby crying, Kane?!" China barked from behind me. Kristine was in her bassinet fussing. I was so caught up in my thoughts of Kristen, I tuned her out. It wasn't like she was wailing or anything.

"I didn't hear her," I replied, trying to make it to the baby before she did.

"Don't try to get up now. Stay over there and continue with your private calls." I stopped in my tracks to talk myself out of backhanding her. That talk lasted all of a half a minute before I grabbed her by the back of her neck.

"You know, ever since this whole shit went down, you've been real flip at the lip. Please don't make me snap ya fuckin' neck." Pushing her towards the bassinet, she stumbled. Recovering quickly, she picked the baby up. Likely thinking that would stop me from going upside her head.

"Do you even want us here? I mean, be honest." China knew she was safe from any physical consequences while she had the baby in her arms, so she spoke freely. "Ever since that bitch was snatched up outta here, you've been beating me from sunup to sundown. Even though you promised the last time was the last time. Why don't you go get your other recruit and knock her fucking lights out, cause I've had it!"

I cracked my neck and knuckles before making my way towards her. She flinched and scurried off before I could do anything. This was the reason I always felt the need to put my hand on these females. They never knew when enough was enough. And my tolerance for women with too much lip had been low since I could remember.

My father had always taught me, *if you allowed a woman the space to talk to you any kind of way, she'd lose respect for you.* And if it was anything that I demanded at all times, it was respect. Her mentioning my other recruit reminded me that I had to pay Chloe a visit. I guess threatening her child did nothing because she still decided to cross me. Grabbing my car keys and phone, I headed for the door. I'd deal with China's ass later.

I needed some pussy. China had been holding out since walking in on me and Kristen, so Ms. Chloe was the next best thing. And one thing about Chloe, she loved this dick. Arriving at her apartment door, I knocked hard. It took her a minute to answer and when she did, she looked spooked.

"Don't look so surprised, baby." I kissed the side of her lips before side stepping her and walking into the apartment like I paid the bills. Waiting for her to close the door, I made myself comfortable on the couch.

"Umm, hey, Kane. I wasn't expecting you," she spoke in a nervous tone.

"I know, I was in the neighborhood. Were you expecting someone else?"

"Kane, you live on the other side of town."

"Yea, but now I'm on your side. It's really quiet in here, where's little Bre?"

"She's with her dad. I'm just resting today."

"Hmph, speaking of your daughter's father." I watched as she shifted back and forth. "I know you let him in the house to get Kristen. My initial reaction was to come here and put my hands on you, but I'm having a change of heart." I decided I could use Chloe in other ways. So, the best thing for me to do right now was to slowly chip at the fear she had of me.

Tired of her standing in her own apartment, I waved her over to sit next to me. Chloe was very pretty. It was her body that did it for me though. Her round titties and peach shaped ass made my dick stand attention whenever I was around her. Pushing her back a little on the couch, I rubbed her pussy through the leggings she had on. She tried to push me away, but I popped her hand.

"Take these off," I demanded. Tapping her leg, she lifted up enough for me to pull the leggings off her.

It didn't take me long to drop my pants to my ankles. Doing the same with my briefs, I sat back down and stroke my dick until it was at its full eight inches. She got on board quickly. Swinging one leg over mine, she lowered herself onto me and my dick massaged her happy place.

"Mmm," we both moaned in satisfaction of the first

stroke. My lips attacked her neck as she slowly bounced up and down on my length, sensually.

"Ughhh, yess Kane, gimmie this dick." She didn't have to tell me twice. Spreading her ass cheeks, I dug off in her, making her scream out. The pussy was gripping so good I almost lost control.

"Yea, I know you missed this dick. I almost didn't give you none for being a bad girl. I got something for you though." I smacked her ass hard and pulled out as I felt her muscles contracting. Lifting her up so that her pussy was at eye level, I put her leg up on my shoulder and used my finger and tongue to make her pussy cream.

"Oooh yeah, shit wait," she begged, her voice going up another octave. By the time she was done cumming, her legs were still shaking as she held onto me.

"We're not done, sweetheart. I haven't given you your punishment yet." I carried her to the bedroom where I wore her ass out like I was on the little blue pill. Afterward, she laid under me with her leg wrapped around my waist.

"What is it that you see in Kristen that you don't see in me or China?" The question was one that I often pondered, yet the answer was always the same.

"She's my soulmate. And without my soul, I'm the heartless man that lies next to you." She sat up to look in my eyes. "Just think of how bad I'd be if her love wasn't something I looked forward to."

"How come you didn't do right by her when y'all were

together? I mean, if you love her the way you say you do, why was it hard to do right?"

I gave her a dead look and I felt her trying to slip free of my embrace. Chloe had learned by now that women were only allowed but so much room to speak their minds when it came to me. She had asked a valid question, though.

"Who said I did wrong? Every man cheats, Chloe. And every now and then, I may have to put my foot up yo ass in order for you to get some act right. It doesn't mean I love you any less. Did I overdo it sometimes with Kristen? Sure, but I plan on changing that once she's back. And she **will** be back." I got out of bed, leaving her stuck. If she thought what I'd done thus far was crazy, what I was prepared to do in the name of love was gonna knock her off her feet.

Ant

It had been a couple days since I'd seen Kristen. After returning home from the park with Bre, she was gone and so was some of her stuff. The crazy thing was, she'd texted me to let me know she was at her parent's crib. Something about needing space to clear her mind. Whatever the fuck that meant. She must've thought I was boo boo the fool. She and I both knew that she needed an excuse to get away to have the abortion done.

What she didn't understand was that I heard her out about not wanting to have the baby. My issue was that she never took my feelings into consideration. Neither one of us knew if the baby was one hundred percent Kane's. She had conveniently forgot that I had been digging her guts out daily since the first time we had sex. Not to mention we were together the night before she was kidnapped. I remembered the night very well. I had almost pulled a damn muscle tryna hit her with the Doug E. Fresh move in the front seat of my Porsche. Overall, I felt like she was being unreasonable.

"Boy, getcho damn feet off my coffee table," my mom scolded me, smacking my foot with a magazine. "How long you plan on sweeping my floor with your bottom lip?"

"What?" She blew me with these ol' country ass analogies.

"How long you plan on walking around here with the long face, dummy?"

"Why I gotta be all that, ma?" I sat up straight on the couch and pulled my hoodie over my head.

"I'm sorry, son, but you and this sad face are sucking all the life out my bachelorette pad."

"Ma, this ain't no damn bachelorette pad. Yo granddaughter always here and you have two more and a possible third that will be running around here behind her soon."

"That's fine. They gon' learn the term, *hot granny summer* real quick. And last I checked, Tremaine has a daughter on the way and a son that I'm still on the fence about. Where does the third baby fit in?"

"Kris is pregnant." I waited for some type of reaction but got nothing. "I said, Kris is pregnant."

"And I heard you. I'm tryna figure out whether I should

be excited or not. By the way you been moving around here, it seems like you don't know either."

"It's not like that." I laid my head back and sighed.

"Well, tell me how it is then. And if you even so much as stretch yo foot out like you wanna put it on my table, I'ma beat you like you stole something." I cracked up at her reading my mind. She already knew about Kristen being kidnapped, so I told her about Kane taking advantage and her becoming pregnant.

"Antwon, as a woman, I fully understand where she's coming from." I went to object, but she held her hand up for me to stand down. "Let me finish. I understand your side as well, son. Have you asked yourself what would become of your relationship if the baby turned out *not* to be yours?" Before I could respond with an answer, my phone rang.

"Yo?"

"Ant, I just spotted dude coming out of your baby mama's crib. You want me to follow him?" The detail I had sitting outside of Chloe's apartment building questioned.

"Yes and be sure to let me know any other stops he makes."

"It's done." The line went dead, and I hopped up. I needed to drop in on Chloe's brick head ass.

"Ma..."

"I know, son, go do what you gotta do and be safe. I'm gonna call Kristen and Kaia a little later to check on them." It sounded like a good idea to me. I kissed her cheek and left out. Just as I was pulling out of the driveway, Maine was pulling in. I stuck my head out the window and he did the same.

"Where you headed?"

"Chloe's crib, you ridin'?"

"You got a lead on the boy in blue?" I nodded. "Aight, I'ma follow you."

He backed out, allowing me to pull out ahead of him. Chloe was steady playing with fire, and I was gon' be the one to burn that ass. I hadn't sent Bre back home since leaving her outside the night I picked up Kristen. Once Kane threatened my seed and she neglected to tell me, she had willingly forfeited her parental rights. To make matters worse, she was still fucking with him.

"Come on, I just wanna ask her a couple questions, then get her to sign over full custody of BreAnn." I showed Maine the paperwork I had Klein draw up for me.

"Sheesh, you think she gon' sign them?"

"It's either that or end up on the ten o'clock news. With the way she's been moving, there's no in between." I knocked on the door and she opened it immediately. I guess she thought ol' boy had doubled back. She wasn't too happy to see the Brown brothers at her door.

"Hmph, Antwon." She spoke, completely ignoring Maine. I'm sure he didn't give a fuck.

"Chloe," I responded with the same energy. "Can we

come in?" She didn't respond with words. Instead, she gestured with her hand, allowing us entry.

"I see you don't have my daughter with you, so I'm not sure why you're here." She tightened the robe she had on and crossed her arms across her chest.

"Yea, we'll get to that in a minute. This is not a social visit. Do you have any info on Kane's whereabouts?"

"I don't," she answered quickly, lying.

"So, he hasn't been here at all?"

"Nope." I shook my head at her ignorance. If she wanted to stick to her lie, I was gonna let her drag herself. At the end of the day, she could get it just like him if that was the side she'd chosen.

"Final answer?" She kept a straight face. "Okay, well before we get going, I need you to sign these papers." Handing them to her, I gave her a minute to look over them.

"Need a pen?" Maine chimed in to piss her off.

"No, I don't need a fucking pen because I ain't signing it. This shit is bogus, and you know it. I'm a good mother, Antwon!"

"As of late, I'm not so sure. And you don't have to sign it willingly, that won't stop the process from happening."

"Over my dead body," she spat venom.

"That will be arranged." Chloe would soon realize that fucking with me would prove to be bad for her health.

"WE GOTTA GET at this nigga, so we can go about our normal day to day, bro." Maine said as we left Chloe's place.

"I'm already knowing. Hol' up, this a message from the detail I put on him." I played the video that was sent to me and watched as Kane picked the lock of Kris's shop and went inside. It was another few minutes before he came back out, looked both ways, and bopped back to his car. The detail followed him to another address where he let himself in. The video stopped there. The text attached stated he hadn't left that address.

"Got 'em, that's where he rests his head for sure. When we moving?"

Maine was hype and so was I. Only I had internalized it because the pain I planned on inflicting on Kane would make that nigga wish he never met Kristen. While I was focused on making Kane a distant memory, I felt a little off. My thoughts kept wandering to the baby situation with Kris.

As if she was somewhere reading my mind, a text message from her came through.

Wife: Hey, we need to talk. Can you stop by my parent's place when you get a chance?

Me: I was thinking the same thing. I'll be by in forty-five minutes. Sliding my phone back into my pocket, I let Maine know my next move before we went our separate ways.

Look, runnin' through this money while your hair is in the wind, Hollywood nights in a drop top Benz, somethin' like my home and my lover and a friend, I was on a roll you another win,

used to be the girl I always said that I'ma get, I remember tellin'
other people in the Benz like when you see... tell her Young Nip got
a APB for her.

My system played Nipsey Hussle's verse off Eric Bellinger's "That's Why" as I cruised towards Kristen's parent's house. Nipsey talked on the record and didn't even say much other than, I been peeping shorty swag and I'm on that. The nigga really had a way with words. The music had me zoned out and made me think about Maine and his career. My brother was a fucking star, and I knew he'd be touching stadiums sooner than later. Unfortunately, I couldn't be as hands on with his career at the moment. Once Kane was in the dirt, we were going harder than before. I made it to my destination in a little under the forty-five minutes I allotted. As I walked up the steps, Kaia was coming down.

"Dayumm," I dragged. "Sis, you getting swollen," I joked, and she rolled her eyes.

"Don't make me cuss yo ass out. This baby keep crip walkin' on my bladder and I'm not in the mood." It seemed her stomach had grown even more overnight.

"You mean as shit, girl. Where you headed?"

"If you must know, I'm going to meet up with ya brother. We have to get the venue paid for the baby shower. Get out my business, though." She mushed me while I laughed, watching her waddle down the steps. My niece was gonna be a problem with her and Maine as parents. Heading inside, I found Kris sitting in the living room.

"What you got going on?" I kissed her forehead and sat down next to her.

"Hey, I'm just looking at the new floor plan for the shop. Thanks for coming by." Turning to face me, she put one of her legs on the couch, exposing a meaty thigh. Sticking to the task at hand, I diverted my eyes to her face. "So, I know I haven't been the best person to deal with since my whole ordeal and for that, I apologize. I know you've been doing more than your best to take care of me both mentally and physically. About this baby, though, I can't keep it, Antwon. How could I give birth to a child that may be an extension of the person I despise?"

I sighed. "I hear you, but you haven't considered the other side of this, my side. What if the baby is mine? It'll be a child we know was made out of love."

"And if it's not yours, what does that mean for us, Antwon?" I paused. I knew for sure that I could never have ill feelings for a child that didn't ask to be born, but I also knew it would fuck me up to know that she'd birthed Kane's seed.

Still, I responded with how I felt at the moment. "We'll cross that bridge when we get there. I need you to hold it down though because you and I both know how I feel about kids." She put her head down, defeated. "Ay, don't do that. Didn't I say I got you, I got us." I picked her head up and leaned in to kiss her lips. She shied away at first, but deepened the kiss as I massaged her thigh.

"Umm, excuse me daughter and son in law, don't y'all have somewhere else y'all can go to swap spit?" We pulled away from each other at the sound of her mother's voice. Kris held her forehead against mine, and I laughed.

"Sorry bout that Ma dukes." I got up to hug her with Kris doing the same.

"Mmhmm, did y'all get a chance to talk about the baby?"

"We did and we came to an understanding," I answered for the both of us. At least I felt like we came to an understanding. Something in me felt strongly that the baby Kristen was carrying was mine, so I was sticking with that feeling.

Kaia

This pregnancy was officially starting to kick my ass and it made sense now that I was nearing the end. My back hurt, my ass had spread wider, and I was irritable. I hadn't seen much of Maine after finding out he was the father of Kandice's son. He would pop up on me every now and then, but most of our communication was via text. No matter how tough I appeared to be, I was missing his presence. I wouldn't admit it out loud, though.

Pulling up to the venue in Westchester, I sent him a text to let him know that I had arrived. He responded that he was already inside taking a tour of the place. I got out to check it out myself. The space I rented held two hundred people max.

It was more than enough space for the festivities, because I only planned on inviting fifty people from my side and Maine's mean ass didn't have many friends.

"Hi, welcome to Create a Space. I'm Liz, you must be Kaia."

"I am, how'd you know it was me?"

"Well honey, other than you being my only four o' clock appointment, your boyfriend described you to a tee."

"I see." I didn't know why Maine was out here false claiming. Even though I thought it was cute.

"Right this way. And might I say you're carrying your pregnancy very well." I thanked her and followed her to the next room. Without my permission, my heart did a back flip when I saw Maine talking to who I assumed was one of the other event coordinators. I braced myself for him to embrace me. I cleared my throat, and he turned around and walked my way. Damn, why his swag had to be so crazy? I stayed poise on the outside, but on the inside, I was putty.

"Hey, daddy's baby," he spoke to my belly. I sucked my teeth with my jealous ass. "Don't be jealous of my daughter." He chuckled and so did the coordinator.

We took about twenty minutes to tour the place and I made sure to record it so that I could send it in my group chat. The girls were in charge of décor. I just wanted to be able to pick the place. After Maine paid and we both signed off on the rental space, I made my way back to my car. As I walked, I felt a sharp pain in my side.

"Ohh," I groaned as another one hit me before I was able to fully recover from the first one. "Owww." Putting my hand on the door of the car next to mine to hold myself up, I bent over and took deep breaths, hoping the pain would ease up.

"Ay, you good?" Maine came up beside me, grabbing hold of my hand. "Why you ain't call out my name? I was right back there."

"I'm good. I think it was one of those Braxton Hicks contractions, thanks." I went to walk again, and he stopped in front of me, placing his hand on my belly.

"Hey Princess, it's daddy. I need you to take it easy on mommy, we're almost to the finish line." I blinked back tears.

"Your voice must be soothing to her. Whenever you talk, she seems to take it easy on me."

"She's daddy's baby that's why. How you been feeling?"

"You know you ask me that every day, right?" His lip curled up and he shook his head.

"Never mind then, Kaia. Come on, let me help you in the car. I need to go pick up my son." I didn't mean to come off harsh, but he sure got my ass by mentioning his son. I high-tailed it to my car so he wouldn't see the tears coming from my eyes. "Kaia, hold up, ma." I didn't bother turning around. Opening the door, I had one foot in before he stopped me.

"I'm good, Tremaine. Let me get home, I'm tired."

"What we doing here, shorty?"

"I'm going home and you going to get ya son remember," I responded sarcastically.

"You know I didn't mean anything by it. I miss the fuck out you man and every time I'm around you, you act like you can't get away from me fast enough. I hate the way we are right now."

"I miss you, too," I admitted. I missed him more than I cared to admit.

"Stay the night with me. I need to have you next to me."

He pushed my wild hair from my face and kissed my lips. Falling victim to his charm and the aching between my legs, I agreed. As I drove behind him, I thought about changing my mind. Again, the baby situation clouded my thoughts. Using my Bluetooth, I set my phone up to call Mecca on Facetime.

"Hey, boo."

"Talk me off the ledge."

"Oh Lord, what happened? Wait, let me close this nail polish because if you make me mess up my toes, I'ma have a real attitude." I glanced at the phone and sure enough her toes and part of her face was in the camera. "Okay, what's tea?"

"I'm on my way to Maine's house. He asked me to stay the night." She didn't respond immediately; in fact, she hadn't moved. "You still there?" I asked, thinking I had poor reception.

"Yes, I'm still here. I was tryna stay still so you would think we had a bad connection and hang up. You so damn dramatic, I swear. That's yo baby daddy, Kaia. Go let that man blow yo back out, rub yo feet, and kiss on yo belly."

"That just makes things more complicated, don't you think?"

"For who? Girl, *you* the only one making things complicated."

"Me?!" It seemed like everyone was forgetting that Maine was the one with a whole other family. First my parents, now Mecca.

"Yes, *you*. Look, I'ma keep it real with you, you're being unreasonable." I wanted to say unreasonable my ass, but I let her continue. "Maine having a baby with someone else can only affect your relationship if you allow it to. He didn't have that baby on you, and he didn't fuck around on you with Kandice. All of that predates y'all relationship. You and I both know you love him, so y'all need to have a conversation that includes setting boundaries for Kandice." I stayed quiet because she was right. It still didn't lessen the sting of my man having a child with a bitch I couldn't stand. "You need to figure out whether it's him having another baby that's the issue or just who he had the baby with. Now, I gotta go... my boo just walked in and we bout to get faded and X-rated. Love you."

She blew a kiss at the phone before hanging up. I called her to put things into perspective and found myself deeper in my feelings. Pulling up behind Maine, I decided it was what it was gon' be.

Inside his apartment, I went straight to Kymani's room to see his progress. The door now had her name on it with star graphics around it for a special touch. Inside, there was a bunch of boxes from different clothing stores in the middle of the floor and all of the furniture was in place. A small couch and love seat were set up along with her crib and matching changing table.

"I need to feel you," he whispered in my ear, making my knees buckle slightly. Taking a handful of my hair, he pulled my head back and latched onto my neck. The seat of my thong got stickier as he nibbled and sucked on my neck.

"Mmm," I moaned while grinding my ass into him.

"You gon' keep dry humping me or you gon' come show me how much you miss this dick?" Turning around, I licked his lips and reached down into his pants to grab a hand full of his thick dick.

"That depends, are you gonna make this pussy cream?"

"You already know I plan on having you walking funny, scouts honor." He held his hand up like a boy scout, making me giggle.

In the bedroom, I stripped down to my thong and bent over, giving him a shot of pussy. I couldn't be as flexible with the belly and all, but I planned on taking all nine inches of that dick. Pulling the thong to the side, I played with my kitty while bouncing my ass in the air. Before I could get caught up in the pleasure I was bringing myself, I felt his tongue slither down my pussy lips.

"Yesss, Maine," I shuddered at the feeling of his thick tongue against my clit. He slurped at my pussy, pulling my clit into his mouth, and humming on it. I couldn't help but to rock back and forth on his face. "Ooh, it's so good, baby," I let out. When I felt his finger slide into my asshole and the sucking on my clit intensified, I lost it. Putting my face in the pillow, I muffled my screams as my pussy exploded.

Not giving me a chance to recover, he entered me slowly. "Arghh fuck, this pregnant pussy ain't nothing but the devil. Goddamn Kaia, lemme see you throw that ass in a circle. Arch that back for me." Doing as he asked, I put a deep arch in my back and threw my ass back.

"Oh God, yess!" I screamed out in pure ecstasy, loud enough to wake up the people on the next floor.

"You wanted me to make this pussy cream, right? I'm keepin' my word." He smacked my ass hard, and the flood gates opened again. I felt him stiffen, letting me know he was right behind me. He released so much, it dripped down my leg as I shivered in delight.

We were settled down after he wiped me off and I still felt like I was coming down off of an unexplainable high. As we cuddled, all that could be heard was the breeze from the cracked window. The sun had settled, and the night sky looked exceptionally beautiful through his sheer curtains. I welcomed the silence as I relished in the moment that I didn't think that we'd have again.

"I'm sorry I hurt you," he broke the silence. "And if I'm continuing to do so, just know it was never my intention. I love you, Kaia. I don't know when and how I fell so fast, but I did. I need you to know that me being a father to my son won't drive a wedge between us going forward. I can't be in a relationship like that, bae." I stayed tight lipped a few seconds in fear that the conversation would take us two steps back.

"I love you, too, Maine. And even though this is hard for me, the best that I can do is try. The last thing I want to do is make you feel that you can't be a father to your son." I turned to face him. "I admire you for that. As far as Kandice goes, it's too far gone for us to even have a conversation at this point. So as long as she doesn't swerve out her lane, I'm good."

"That's all I ask." Placing a wet kiss on my lips, we eventually fell asleep. Tonight would be the first night in my pregnancy that I slept without tossing and turning. Kymani gave me a break from her normal night workout routine. It felt good to sleep up under my man again.

WAKING up the next morning with Maine's arms wrapped around me I felt refreshed and hopeful. The feeling was short lived when I heard loud banging on the front door. I started to get up, but with my round self, I knew he'd get there before me. I nudged him twice, and he didn't budge.

"Babe, you don't hear someone banging on the door. You want me to answer it?"

"Nah, they'll go away," he groaned in a sleepy tone.

Unfortunately for him, the person on the other end was insistent on coming in because the banging continued.

"Tremaine, get up. You don't live in the hood and whoever's at the door ain't leaving. Come on, babe, it might be an emergency." Annoyed, he snatched the sheets off him and got out of bed. I licked my lips while watching his semi-hard dick swing freely.

"Stop lookin' at my dick, Kaia. You ain't tryna get fucked, you want me to answer the door for the emergency." He used air quotes, and I cracked up laughing. Slipping on his boxers and a t-shirt, he stormed out of the room. "It better be an emergency alright, somebody better be on fucking fire!" I got a kick out of him fussing out loud. He was pissed. "Who the fuck is it?!" He barked at the door.

Grabbing one of his shirts from the drawer, along with a pair of shorts, I stepped out into the hallway to be nosey. With his apartment having an open floor plan, I was able to see Kandice standing in the doorway with a baby stroller. I instantly got pissed. *How the hell does she know where he lived?* I thought to myself while walking further out to make my presence known.

"This how you starting off fatherhood? You can't keep ya word? You were supposed to pick your son up yesterday or did you conveniently forget?" One look past him and her eyes collided with mine. "Oh, I see, once again you made yo bitch a priority and not yo son, typical."

"Yo, watch ya mouth in front of him and don't disrespect

my lady." He checked her before I came out of my body. "Now, come inside so we can talk like adults or leave him and go about the rest of your day." Taking the stroller from her, he rolled the baby in. I was hoping she took the latter but of course she jumped at the chance to come inside. I grimaced and grilled him because he was still in his boxers. "My bad, bae, let me go change."

"Yea, you go do that." He headed back to the room, and I watched Kandice's eyes follow. Stepping directly in her line of vision, I cocked my head to the side.

"Don't be threatened by little ol' me. He don't have nothing that I ain't seen." She called herself taking a shot.

"I do, though. I have a fist that hasn't met your eye yet. I'm sure they'll be introduced real soon. Keep it up and I'ma knock the bump right out yo fuckin' bob."

She smirked. "Oh, you real bothered."

"By a bitch who had to fight for the sperm, neva, babes."

"Aight look, we need to establish some boundaries," Maine announced once he returned, looking decent in a pair of basketball shorts. The baby started to cry and he picked him up from the stroller. "Let's start with you popping up to my crib. How you even know where I live?"

"My cousin works at the DMV. When you didn't respond to my calls yesterday, I had her look you up." She shrugged as if it wasn't a big deal. "That's not the point though. The point is that you didn't keep your word to your son!"

"Lower your tone in my house. He's a damn infant, he

don't know what I'm keeping or not keeping. I got side-tracked and didn't get to reach out to you, my bad. But you got me fucked up thinkin' you bout to dictate the way a nigga move. Going forward, I will meet you to pick him up. This popping up at my crib shit is dead, so make it your last time doing it. I don't know how I can make it any clearer that I don't fuck witchu. The only dealings we have is off the strength of him. As far as my woman goes, dead the disrespect cause she ain't going nowhere, which means she will be around him when I have him."

I stood off to the side, watching their interaction, with hatred running all through my body. A blind man could see that Kandice had feelings for Maine and this baby was a way of ensuring he stuck around. One thing for sure and two things for certain, there were no slip ups with me when it came to this bitch. The minute I felt something fishy was going on, I was fucking her and Maine up. I noticed that the baby hadn't so much as squirmed since Maine had picked him up. He really had the magic touch. The baby was a cutie with Maine's complexion and round, alert eyes. I couldn't help but to reach out to touch his hand.

"Unh, unh, that's what we not doing," Kandice interjected.

"Excuse me?"

"Yea, what you mean by that?" Maine added.

"I mean I didn't see her wash her hands and there's a lot of viruses going around. You can never be too careful."

"Bruh, you sound dumb as hell. You didn't see me wash my hands either." Maine defended me and I shook my head at her ignorance.

"It's okay, bae, I'ma be in the room. Stupidity is contagious, too, and I don't want to catch it." It wasn't too long before I heard them going back and forth and the door slam.

A minute later, he was back in the bed and pulling me close to him.

"Where's the baby?"

"Her silly ass took him. I should've listened to my mama when she said to watch who I stuck this big motherfucka in."

"Unh, unh move." I pushed him off me and he laughed. "You know damn well that's not what she said."

"You right, she actually said lil thang, but you and I both know that's inaccurate." I squeezed my legs tight, thinking about the things he did to my body last night. "My sentiments exactly." I threw a pillow at his cocky ass.

"On a serious note, though. You better keep yo baby mama in check. If she keeps going with her bullshit, I can guarantee I'm gonna tag her ass when I drop or put one of the girls on it." The ass whooping was years in the making anyway.

"I'm handling it and it's not gonna affect us. Come on, let's get dressed since we're up now. We can go eat breakfast at my mom's house. She texted me and she wants to see you." I heard food and was showered and dressed in fifteen minutes flat.

"Slow down, there's gonna be food left when we get there," he clowned as we walked to the car.

"That's not even funny." I pouted.

"Aww, come here." He wrapped his arms around my waist and kiss my lips twice. "I'm sorry, big mama. You can eat all the food you want, even mine." He smiled.

"You annoying," I giggled. "Move back and open the door." Pushing him with my belly, he opened the passenger door to the car and helped me in.

"I just know that seat happy as hell. That ass is sitting up nice." Grinning, I closed the door and put my seatbelt on.

Twisting the seatbelt in a position comfortable for me and my belly, I took out my phone to text Kristen. Before I could scroll to our thread, an incoming FaceTime call from Shanice came through.

"Hey pooh, talk to me nice." That was code for, *my man in the car, watch what you say.*

"Hey, big mama. I was just calling to show you seat cover options for the shower."

"I like whatever y'all like. I know it's not gonna look crazy so just choose."

"Good choice, boo. You got a lil' glow and it ain't the pregnancy." She scrunched her face up, making me giggle. **"You got some cuddy last night."**

I smirked and nodded while putting up three fingers to indicate three times.

"Four," Maine made his way into my conversation. "I hit

you once while you were sleeping." I side eyed him and Shanice cracked up.

"**Bye Sha.**"

"**Love you, too, best friend,**" she replied before hanging up. The closer we got to Ma Janes the more excited I got.

"That's a damn shame, shorty. You really dancing about food?"

"Shut up and drive." I was on a high. Me and my baby had made up and I was about to stuff my face. All was right with the world.

Maine

After a continuous battle, I had finally come up with a decent schedule for me to spend time with Chase. Even after coming to an agreement, Kandice found something to complain about every chance she got. Each time I went to pick him up, she had a new complaint and somehow it always involved Kaia, whether she was around or not. Usually, that shit went in one ear and out the other, but then there were times when I had to go in on her, and she'd shut up real quick. Today was no different. I'd dropped Chase off an hour ago after having him overnight and hadn't stepped foot in my place before she was calling.

"What man, damn?" I spoke in aggravation through my AirPods.

"Why you couldn't keep him another night?"

"Because today is my baby shower, and you know that. I'll be back to get him tomorrow."

"Whatever, Maine. That other baby ain't get here yet, he's here now. You need to spend as much time with him as possible."

"I don't move on your time, Kandice. Get that through your thick ass skull." I banged it on her simple ass. I wasn't about to go back and forth, that only made her think she was more important that she was.

"Bae, that's you?" Kaia yelled from the back.

"Yea, who else you think got the key to my place?"

"Shut up, here... this is for you to put on." She walked out in her panties and bra, with a big ass pacifier for me to put around my neck.

"Oh nah, I don't see you with a goofy ass accessory. I'm not putting that shit on." She giggled but my face remained serious.

"Babeee, come on, stop playing. This is gonna let everybody know you the daddy."

"Everybody know that already and if they don't, then we need to be planning your homegoing and not getting ready for a baby shower." I gave her a dead stare and she sucked her teeth. "Something you wanna say?"

"Nothing other than, you sure know how to ruin a party."

I chuckled. "Yea, yea. Let's get dressed before we're late."

I smacked her ass and followed her to the bedroom where she had clothes laid out on the bed for the both of us. We were doing all white Givenchy. For me, a white Givenchy polo with the logo on the sleeves and a pair of white distressed jeans. My baby turned shit up a notch when she stepped out in an all-white Givenchy jumpsuit.

"You lookin' all good and shit. Let's go before you have to find another outfit."

Knowing what I was capable of, she practically skipped to the door, and I laughed, walking out behind her. When we pulled up, Mecca was outside with a headset around her head like she was a real event planner. I didn't wanna laugh because she was taking her job very seriously, escorting us in through a side door, so no one would see us. It was funny how the first baby shower I'd ever been to was my own. Both of our families got along well, and it was one big party. After playing multiple games at Heaven's direction and everyone was full off the buffet style meal the hall had set up, it was time to open gifts.

"Alright now, gather around cause it's y'all time to shine. All big bag givers to the front, and all diaper and wipe givers to the bizack," Mecca announced.

"Mecca!" Kaia swatted her.

"Okay, I'm just playin'. But on a serious note, you only get one chance to claim your gift once the parents show it. If you don't claim it, then it's from me." Everyone bust out laughing as they took their seats.

Kaia and I sat in chairs that were shaped like thrones and prepared to open up what looked like a sea of gifts. Just as Mecca went to hand Kaia the first bag, shots rang out. Kaia dropped to the ground and as I went to dive on top of her, I watched Mecca's body jerk before she fell. I couldn't even think as adults and children scrambled to get to a safe area in the hall. There were a few more shots before they ceased.

Jumping up once they stopped, there was pandemonium all around me.

"Tremaine, get off of me, I gotta check on Mecca." Kaia fought to push me off her.

"Meccaaaaaa! No, not my baby." I watched as Mecca's mother, Shanice, and her mother ran over.

Kristen and Ms. Diane brought up the rear. While Kaia fought to get out of my grasp, I was too busy checking to make sure she wasn't hurt.

"I'm fine, Tremaine. Let me go." She snatched away from me and slowly walked over to the group of women that were huddled around Mecca.

I went to run outside and made it to the hallway, just as Dino rushed back in with his gun at his side.

"What happened? Did you see anybody?"

"Nah, just the car as it sped off. I was able to let two shots off that hit the back window."

"What kinda car was it?"

"A tan Ford Focus."

"You get the plate?"

"Nah. I just saw that shit speeding and got to dumping."

"Damn, aight. Let me go back in here and calm every-body down, then we ride out."

Pissed that I didn't have a license plate or the face behind the hit, I stormed back inside. There was only one person that could've been the cause of this mayhem. The commotion had died down a little, but cries could still be heard throughout the hall as everyone shuffled to leave. One cry in particular pierced my ears.

"Nooo, no, no Mecca, please!" I heard Kaia's grief-stricken voice as I made my way through the crowd.

When I reached her, tears were streaming down her beautiful face. Her clothes were painted in blood as she cradled Mecca in her arms while Shanice held her hand with a blank stare. The other women were doing their best to console Mecca's mother. I knew she was gone. Her eyes were open but void of any signs of life. I hung my head in despair and cautiously walked over to them. Hearing sirens in the distance, I knew someone had called the police. As I got closer, Kaia looked up and shook her head *no*, like she knew what I was about to say.

"I'm not letting her go. She needs me, Maine. I can't leave her like this, babe."

"I know, baby, come on, let the ambulance get her so they can take her to the hospital." Though I knew there was no saving Mecca, I didn't have it in me to tell my baby that. She was adamant about not letting her friend go. Once the EMT's cleared a path, I was able to convince Kaia to let them do their job. Calling Heaven over while Kris grabbed Kaia, I rattled off instructions. "Heaven, I need you to handle this for me. I gotta go find out who did this shit. Tell the owner all damage will be paid for. Whatever the bill is tell her to email Kaia. And please, please make sure my babies are straight." I stressed, referring to Kaia and our unborn.

"I got it, go."

Leaving out, I stopped to kiss Kaia's head and whispered that I loved her.

"Hey, Maine," Kristen called out, "please tell Ant to call me. He went to find your mom outside before the shooting started. Now he's not answering the phone."

"I got you, sis." I nodded to Dino, and we left out.

As we made it to the door, Mase was running in.

"What the fuck is going on? I'm on the phone with Diane, on my way here, and I heard gunshots. Tell me something, Maine." He gave me a hard look.

"I really don't have much information, man. But I will soon enough. Right now, they need you."

He pinched the bridge of his nose and closed his eyes. "Is my family okay?"

"Yea...but—."

"Make it right, Maine. I'm holding you to that. Trust, I'm

willing to take it there behind my family. Make it right." I nodded, and he rushed into the hall.

Wanting to be gone before the police pulled up with questions, I got out of dodge.

"Yo, where my brother and my mama?" I asked as we hopped inside my car and started it up. Dino was silent and I didn't like that shit at all. I turned the car off and turned to him. "Dawg, right now is not the time to fuck with me."

"Ant took moms to the hospital. She was shot, too," he said solemnly.

"Who moms? Not my motherfuckin' mama! On my fuckin' life dawg, if something happens to Jane Brown, I'm airing out the fucking city! Call Ant and find out what hospital they in."

BEFORE WE GOT with Kaia and Kris, any chaos in our lives stemmed from what we created. In all the years we'd been in the game, we hadn't had any major static. Now that we were forced to go legit everything seemed to be going left. The complete opposite of what we'd left the game for in the first damn place.

Busting through the doors of Westchester Medical, I demanded to see my mother. I tried not to think the worst and the receptionist had better thank her lucky stars for that. Me being worried was nothing nice for anyone around me.

As she looked up my mother's information in the system, I could hear her voice in the distance.

"Y'all can stop fussin' over me. It's just a damn flesh wound."

Rushing to the back where I heard her voice, I could hear the nurse calling out about security, but I didn't give a damn. She could have that orange looking ass President called down to the hospital, wasn't nobody bout to stop me from seeing my mama. Finally finding her sitting in the hallway with a nurse hovering over her, I interrupted.

"Ma," I called out. "You good?"

"She'll be fine," the nurse assured me with a smile while bandaging her up.

"Exactly. Like I said, it's a flesh wound." I was relieved to know that.

"We need to get you home. Shit…" I stopped mid-sentence, seeing that the nurse was still present. "Why is she in the hallway?"

"Cause yo brother went to cuttin' up soon as we got here. Told them that they had better get a doctor to see bout me or shit was gon' go left. I'm surprised they ain't put our ass out."

"Where he at?"

"Over there talking to the doctor. What the hell happened back at the hall and is everyone okay?" I dropped my head as Mecca's dead eyes flashed in my head.

"All set, Ms. Brown. I'm gonna grab some supplies for you to take home and some pain medication."

"Don't need it," we said at the same time.

"Oh," the nurse responded. "Well, okay. I'll just get the supplies." I waited until she was out of earshot to report what happened.

"Everything is not okay. Mecca was hit, too. She didn't make it." She grabbed my hand and squeezed it tightly. "Whoever let the shots off meant them for Kaia, ma. Mecca was standing right in front of her."

"Damn, that poor girl. What the hell is going on?"

"Can't get into that. Just know, we're handling it." Looking up, I saw Ant coming our way and his face matched my feelings.

"You good, ma?" He asked.

"Yes. I'm waiting for the nurse to return with the supplies."

"We're not waiting. I'll have Doc come check you out. Right now, I need to get to Kris' parents' house and we..." he gestured to me, "need to get in the field."

My mother didn't argue. She got up, kissed both of our heads, and started towards the front to leave the hospital. We were about to get our hands dirty, and it was about time.

"Mecca is dead," I let him know as we walked side by side. "Dino saw a Ford Focus speeding out of the parking lot and was able to get two shots off. No plate and no I.D."

"Aight." His response was flat.

Arriving at Kaia's house, I chose not to go inside. I knew that if I did, I'd want to stay and comfort Kaia. Right now, time was no friend of ours, and we couldn't afford to waste another minute not addressing this situation. We needed to make our presence felt. Leaving Dino behind, Ant hopped in my car, and we peeled out.

"This shit with Kane gotta end, man. My girl almost got hit up, and her fucking friend is dead, bro. What was supposed to be a day of celebration, ended in tragedy. I can't go home, look my girl in the eye, and not be able to tell her that she can sleep well because we ended her friend's killer and her sister's rapist." Ant didn't respond with words, but his eyes said we were on the same page.

Our first stop was to the house Kane had Kris held in when he kidnapped her. Night had fallen and the street was eerily quiet as we pulled into the development. We didn't have to get out the car to know that he was no longer there. The for-sale sign confirmed it. Luckily, Ant still had the text from the detail he had on Kane. Hoping for a better outcome at the other address, we went there.

"Ain't this about a bitch. This motherfucka living real quiet while he going around making a lot of fucking noise in our lives," Ant commented. "I ain't knocking on the door either. I'm kicking that bitch in. I'm tired of playin' with this nigga." The lights were off, but it didn't deter bro from kicking in the door like he said he would. Unfortunately for us, no one appeared to be home. "How the fuck is this nigga a step ahead of us?"

I had to admit, going after this dude had me feeling

incompetent. Every time we were a step closer, he'd slip right through our fingers.

"Dammit. Come on man, let's get outta here." My phone rang in my pocket. Pulling it out, I answered as we jogged back to my car.

"**Yo?**" I listened as Dino spoke and my jaw flexed. "**Get the fuck outta here...aight, man.**" Hanging up, I swung the driver's side door open and tossed my phone in the middle console. "Bro, you ain't gon' believe this shit."

Kane

Pulling the ski mask off my head, I felt a rush as I weaved in and out of traffic. Seeing everyone scrambling for cover from the gunshots had me on a high. I could only hope that the intended targets were hit. Glancing over at my accomplice, I smiled once she removed her mask.

"How you feeling, baby?"

"Like a fucking target. And it don't help that we're riding around with no back window either. I can't believe I shot someone. Oh shit, do you think he saw us? Shit, he saw us. He's gonna kill me. Something told me to go the other way when I met yo ass." I listened to her ramble for a whole mile before pulling over in a seedy neighborhood and turning off the engine.

"Hey! Calmate." I yelled out, telling her to relax in Spanish.

"What? I don't speak Spanish, Kane."

"It means calm down. You're in good hands with me and I promise you those motherfuckas don't know what hit them." I was confident in that. My track record in what I'd been able to get away with thus far spoke for itself. From getting Maine locked up on the drug charge to snatching Kristen up right in front of her shop, then there was today. I was up by three and didn't plan on stopping until their whole family was dismantled and Kristen took her rightful place at my side.

"Why are we stopping?"

"My ride is coming to get me." I hopped out of the car with her on my heels.

"Wait, what ride? Why do you keep springing shit on me? And how the hell am I getting home?" She grabbed at my shirt. I had been getting a little better with my hands, but her persistence had me itching to slap her to the ground.

"I ordered an Uber for you, unless you want your baby daddy to get word that I dropped you off. If so, by all means, ride with me," I answered sarcastically. Just like I thought, she didn't have a comeback. We waited a few minutes before both our rides pulled up at the same time. I opened her door and helped her inside.

"Sir, make sure my lady friend here gets home safe." The

driver nodded and I focused my attention back on the passenger. "It was a pleasure working with you, my dear. Until we meet again, Kandice."

"Yea, well, you better hope that I come out on the winning end of this or you're gonna have some problems. Ya feel me?" I smiled at her weightless threat. Kissing her head, I tapped the roof of the car, and the driver pulled off.

"Just another bitch you adding to the stable, huh?" Chloe stated smartly as I entered the car.

"Don't worry, baby, no one can take your place. She's just a means to an end."

"Yea, and apparently, so am I," she mumbled under her breath. Unfortunately, it was loud enough for me to hear. She didn't see it coming when I slapped her upside her head.

"That's for being a stupid ass bitch. Now, drive the car and shut the fuck up, goddamn! Matta fact move and let me drive." I didn't know who was worse, her or China. I was equally tired of the both of them feeling the need to express their opinion about the moves I made. There was always reasoning behind my decisions. Linking up with Kandice was no different.

I was sitting in the parking lot of the jail where Maine was being held. Through one of my many contacts, I was able to set up a visit with him posing as his attorney. I wanted him to know that even though I was no longer with the department, I still had connections. The goal was to bring Kristen to me by going after what she loved and whoever was attached to that person was a bonus. As I walked up to the building, I took notice of a female who stormed out with a baby in her arms and a scowl on her face. She had a phone pressed to her ear and I could hear her yelling at whoever was on the other end.

"I'm done with this shit. All that nigga care about is Kaia. The plan was to fuck him, make him fall for me, and have his baby. Clearly the plan was a major fail. All I ended up with is a baby attached to me for the next eighteen years, a sore mouth from sucking his dick all the time, and a wet ass. Fuck Tremaine Brown!"

I stopped in my tracks and my eyes zoomed in on the woman scorned. Her venting sparked my interest.

"Hey, I'm sorry to interrupt, but I couldn't help but to overhear your conversation. Do you happen to know someone by the name of Maine?" She curled up her lip and told the person on the other end of the phone that she'd call them back.

"You're very fuckin' nosey to have overheard my conversation. That's my baby daddy, though, who you?"

"Whoever you need me to be to get what you want. Come, let's talk." I abandoned my initial mission, figuring that this would pan out better.

It didn't take much convincing to get Kandice to see things from my perspective. She told me about her history with Kaia and I planted additional seeds to keep that hateful fire burning. Pulling out from the curb, a hit to the side of my head made me swerve into oncoming traffic faster than I wanted to.

"I'm fucking tired of you putting your hands on me, you bastard!" Chloe shrieked.

I tried to regain control of the car and push her off me at the same time, but she'd caught me off guard. Whatever strength she had mustered up had her ready to kill us both. Rearing my hand back, I slapped her hard, and her head hit the passenger side window just as a car collided with ours.

"Oh shittt!" I tried to break before the car spun out of control and into a tree, knocking us both out.

BEEP, *beep, beep.*

I heard the sounds of a machine and knew where I was before I could open my eyes. Flicking them open, I saw China sitting in the corner, bouncing our daughter, Kristine, up and down in her lap. There was a scowl on her face and I already knew why. My head was pounding and when I went to sit up, my arm felt weighed down.

"It's in a cast. Broken, due to the impact of the hit." China clarified things for me, continuing to bounce Kristine up and down with no regard for my current state.

"When did you get here?" I questioned.

"I'm your only emergency contact. Well, besides Kristen, and we both know she ain't coming."

"I see you got jokes. I'll let it slide." Of course I still had

Kristen as my emergency contact. She was even in my last will and testament. China didn't need to know that though.

"Yea, well, you might want to get an updated number for her. Right now, you have to settle for me and your daughter." I went to say something, but a knock at the door made me pause.

"Come in."

"Hi, I'm Dr. Smith, nice to see you up, Mr. Ramirez." A female doctor walked in with a nurse behind her. "The pain meds put you out for a few hours. You have a nasty bruise on your head which should heal in no time. Now this arm is another story. It's been broken in two places so the healing there is gonna be a little more extensive. We've checked out everything else and you're medically cleared to go home. I'm gonna have the nurse give you a script for pain and instructions on home care." I thanked her and she nodded before turning to leave.

"Oh, Dr. Smith, I was with someone when I got into the accident. Can you tell me how she's doing?" I needed to know if Chloe was alive so that when I was better, I could beat her ass so severely she'd wish she was dead.

"She took quite the beating, but she's doing okay. You take care of yourself." The undertone in her response made me think she was in some way trying to look out for Chloe.

"Hmph, well, I just came by to check on you, but I see it's still fuck China." I turned to China who was now placing the baby in her stroller.

"China, right now, I need you to tuck that attitude away and hang in there with me." My arm temporarily put me out of commission and with Chloe being out as well, I needed China to pick up the slack.

"Hang in there?" She scoffed and came closer to me. "What the fuck you think I've been doing all this time, Kane? I've been sitting home, holding it down while you go out there playing lone ranger. Get it through your fucking head... KRISTEN DOES NOT WANT YOU!!" Grabbing at her face with my good arm, I pulled her close enough for her to smell what I ate the night before.

"I hope you feel better now that you got that off your chest. Please don't let this cast on my arm make you feel that you can't get fucked up. Now, go get those discharge papers so I can get outta here." She went to snatch away from me, but I had a tight grip on her face. "And leave the baby. I wouldn't want you to get any crazy ideas like thinking your leaving me. We both know that's not an option, my love."

I let go and sent her on her way. See, unlike Chloe, China feared me way too much to go any further than trying to assert herself. We'd known each other a while and I knew her weaknesses just as she knew mine. She'd never leave me because she had nobody but me. And while I knew that she loved me deeply, it was the fear that I fed off of.

After another couple hours, I was finally discharged with specific instructions for at home care. I handed China the paperwork to hold and we were on our way. Before leaving, I stopped by the nurse's station to see if I could get any more detailed information on Chloe's condition. I put on my charming smile and got to schmoozing.

"Excuse me, my name is Kane, and I came in with my sister-in-law after a car accident. I wanted to check on her status. So far, I haven't heard anything." The young nurse looked around as if she was looking for someone to answer the question I'd just asked her.

"Umm, sir, I'm not allowed to give you that information under the guidelines of HIPPA." I touched her hand, and she tensed up.

"Miss, I just want to know if she's okay. Please, just let me see her. I'll be quick, I promise." I even dropped a tear for added theatrics.

"Unfuckinbelievable," China murmured, making me turn my head in her direction.

She cast her eyes to the floor, and I turned my attention back to the nurse. Scanning the hallway once more, she waved me over to follow her with a nod of her head. The TV could be heard as I entered room two twelve behind the nurse. In the bed, I found Chloe laid up with a bandage on her head and the hospital sheet up to her neck. Getting close enough for her to sense my presence, I reached for her hand under the sheet.

"I hope you get better sooner than later. We have unfinished business," I whispered in her ear. My voice was calm but deadly. She squeezed her eyes closed tightly and that let me know she heard me. "Thank you for allowing me to see her, Nurse... Connie," I read the name from her name tag. "You have a great day. I'll see you soon, sis, love you."

China begrudgingly helped me to my car, mumbling under her breath the whole time. During the car ride we didn't utter a word to one another. I was thinking about my plans being slightly derailed due to my unforeseen injury. I was also racking my brain about where we could stay after yesterday's event. I didn't put it past the Brown brothers to have already sought out the house where we laid our heads.

"I need to use your phone. I gotta make a few calls and get you and the baby moved somewhere safe."

"Why we gotta move? And where will you be?"

"Because I said so. Don't worry about me." Just as I went to dial a number, her phone ring. The caller ID showed unknown. She glanced over at me while I looked at the phone then to her accusingly. The phone rang four times before I answered.

"**Hello?**" The caller spoke. I didn't let on that the person said anything, instead I just hung up. What the hell was China doing talking to Kristen?

Ant

Not being able to locate Kane was causing an unspoken wedge between Kris and me that neither one of us wanted to acknowledge. She'd also been secret in her movements lately, thus making an already tense situation worse. I was so focused on getting her to shake back from her ordeal that I let Kane slip through my fingers once again. It was like he went down a rabbit hole and I couldn't for the life of me figure out how he was hiding this well.

"Daddy, can I go see mommy?" Bre asked, climbing up in the bed next to me.

I wanted to say, *no I don't want you around that disloyal bitch*, but I knew I couldn't. The most communication I allowed between Bre and Chloe was Facetime and regular calls. Other than that, I still didn't trust her ass. On top of that, she wasn't trying to sign the custody papers. And though there was a plethora of reasons why I wanted to put her ass to sleep, Kristen had convinced me not to.

"Yes, princess. Call her and see if she can meet us at the park tomorrow." I handed her my phone and got up to go to the bathroom. When I was done, I heard a man's voice on the other end of the Facetime call. "Bre, who you talkin' to?"

"Mommy's friend, look daddy." She turned the phone around and Kane's face appeared with a smirk. I snatched the phone from her and rushed out the room.

"**You a real pussy. You still in hiding? Why you can't talk to me face to face?**"

"Oh, I'm not hiding, you're just not looking good enough. How's the family? I heard there was a shooting recently. Is everyone okay?"

"**The best thing for you to do is stay in hiding because when I find, and I *will* find you, I'm going to break every fucking bone in ya body. And tell Chloe she no longer has a daughter.**" I disconnected the call and launched my phone across the room.

"Antwon! What the hell? You're scaring Bre." I turned around to find Kris cradling Bre in her arms, confused.

"This situation you got me in is what the fuck is wrong!" I snapped. "Do you know this motherfucka was just on Facetime with my damn daughter?!" I punched the wall out of frustration, not taking into consideration how scared Bre was.

"It's okay, mamas. Come on, let me take you to your room so you can watch TV." She walked off, consoling Bre while I went in the opposite direction, downstairs to the kitchen. After ten minutes and a shot of henny, Kris came in with her face turned up.

"You ready to have an adult conversation? One that doesn't include you breaking shit." She tossed my broken XS Max on the table.

"Man, go head and let me calm down before I hurt yo feelings."

"You're passed that point already. You think I want this shit to be happening? I LOST SOMEONE THAT WAS LIKE A LITTLE SISTER TO ME, ANTWON! This shit can't be harder on you than it is on me."

"And I almost lost my fuckin' mama so what you saying?!"

"Wow, so now we comparing casualties?"

"I didn't mean it like that. While you in here with all this energy, tell me why the fuck you been sneaking around lately? You plotting with that nigga or something? Probably tellin' him that's his baby and shit."

"My first mind is to punch you in yo shit, but I'ma let you

have that because clearly you're upset. Let's be clear, I don't want nothing to do with this baby. Need I remind you that I'm having it because of **you**. And for the record, you ain't the only one that's tryna get revenge." She turned and left me standing in the kitchen thinking about what she said. *And for the record, you ain't the only one that's tryna get revenge.*

Taking another shot, I made up in my mind that the best thing to do at this point was to get back to stacking bread. The more I thought about it, our success was going to flush Kane out. He expected us to continue playing this cat and mouse game with him, so we were gonna do the exact opposite. It was time for me to get my shit together in order to come out on top of this shit. First thing in the morning, I was getting back to business. Tonight, I had some making up to do.

In the bedroom, I heard water running. Following the sound, I found Kris bent over testing the water temperature as she ran herself a bath. Her belly hadn't fully formed but the pudge was noticeable in her panties and bra. She still went about her day to day as if she wasn't pregnant. That's how disconnected she was. As she stood up, I wrapped my arms around her, strategically placing my hands on her stomach.

"I'm sorry, ma." She just shook her head and moved from my embrace.

"You can go give that apology to BreAnn. She may be more forgiving."

Shit, I ran my hand over my face. I had scared my baby girl. Bre wasn't used to me yelling at her unless she actually did something wrong and even that was rare. In this case, I snapped due to being in my own feelings. Heading to her room, I found her laying at the foot of her bed with her eyes glued to the TV.

"Hey, daddy's baby." I sat next to her, and she kept her eyes straight ahead, not even acknowledging my presence. Yea, I was gonna have to pay. "Daddy sorry for yelling at you, mamas. I was upset and that wasn't right. You forgive me?"

"Yea, daddy. You wanna watch *Peppa Pig* with me?" She looked up at me with a big smile like she just knew she was getting over. I smiled back and nodded.

Getting comfortable on her full-size bed, I watched two episodes with her until she fell asleep. Tucking her in, I went back to my room. Kris wasn't in bed, so I went to look for her in the bathroom. She was just stepping out the tub. She didn't acknowledge it, but the baby growing inside her had her spreading in all the right places. Her thighs had a little more definition to them, and her breasts seemed to swell overnight along with her ass. She may not have liked it, but the baby was doing her body good.

"Stop staring at me." She grabbed her towel from the rack and covered herself up. I had been so focused on her body, I hadn't taken notice of her puffy eyes until she told me to stop staring. Following her into the bedroom, she sat back on the bench in front of the bed with her shoulders hunched over. "Mecca's funeral is in three days."

"I know, shit is fucked up man."

"My sister hasn't even been answering the phone for me, Antwon. I know she thinks it's my fault." I sat next to her and let her put her head on my shoulders.

"It's not your fault, ma. We gon' get through this shit, I promise you that. I was out of line earlier and I apologize. From today forward, we movin' different. After we lay Mecca to rest, we gon' start living again, just more cautious. I'm gon' put someone on you, Kaia, and your parents at all times. We ain't taking no more losses, on God."

THE NEXT MORNING, I called a meeting with my team down at the record company. I had to conference Maine in on the call because he wasn't ready to leave Kaia's side just yet. She had been taking Mecca's death extremely hard, rightfully so.

"Alright, thank y'all for coming today. Maine is unable to be here, but he'll be joining us on a video chat." I dialed Maine in, and his face appeared on the flat screen, in the conference room. "I know I've been out of pocket for a minute, and I wanna thank you all for holding it down in my absence. Today, we're back to business, but we're kicking it into high gear. It's tour time ladies and gentlemen."

I went into detail about the tour line up and what cities

we'd be hitting. Maine would be the headliner, while the other three artists would be the opening acts. So far, they had gained a pretty good following thanks to their talent. I had a promo team set to go up to radio stations to get the records spinning, and a street team to get posters plastered on every available space. I was gonna flush Kane out and make money at the same time.

Kaia

"**G**irl, if I go before you, can you sing Marsha Ambrosius' part to "Real Big" at my funeral? You know they was tryna play my good sis at Nipsey Hussle's funeral like she can't blow," Mecca said as we sat around her house eating snacks and talking about baby names.

"How we go from baby names to dying, Mecca?"

"Right, don't even talk like that," Shanice cosigned while Mecca shrugged her shoulders.

"It was just a random thought. Y'all know I space out sometimes. I'm gon' out live both of y'all hoes anyway." She stuck her tongue out, making me chuckle.

"Y'all know I love y'all, right?" I said, feeling myself get *emotional. "Y'all my sisters forreal, and I wouldn't want to be on this journey without y'all, real shit."*

"Please, don't start crying. We love you, too, Kaia." Shanice got up and put her arms around my neck, and Mecca followed.

"Cause we are sistas, we stand together, we make up one big family, no we don't look the same, our spots are different, different colors." Mecca's singing made us crack up laughing. "I love y'all more."

That was months ago. Today, I was supposed to be preparing to lay my friend to rest, but all I could do was lie in bed and cry. I hadn't spoken much in the past few days, nor did I have much of an appetite. Mecca laying in my arms as she took her last breath was now tattooed on my brain. I tried to sleep as much as I could so that I could at least dream of good times with my best friend. When I was up, my mind drifted to the bullets that hit her that I was sure were meant for me. I knew I wasn't in the running for mommy of the year the way I'd been slacking on taking care of myself.

"Babe, come on, we gotta start getting ready. The service starts at twelve, it's nine." Maine stood over me in a sweatsuit with the hoodie over his head. I had been staying at my parents' house since the shooting and Maine had made their guest room that doubled as an office his own bedroom. Not only was he there for me, but he wanted to ensure I was at least doing the minimum to make sure his baby remained on a healthy path to delivery.

"I can't do it, Maine. It's just gonna make everything seem

so real. If I go and watch her be put in the ground today that means I'm saying goodbye, and I don't wanna do that, bae." The tears streamed down my puffy cheeks at a rapid pace. My eyes were so swollen from crying that I'm sure it looked like allergies had gotten the best of me.

"I know it's hard, shorty, but think about her mom and Shanice, they're gonna need you there. And you know Mecca would want you to celebrate her life not mourn her this way."

"What life, Maine? Her fucking life was stolen from her! There's nothing to celebrate. She was supposed to be here! I don't wanna bury my friend."

Instead of getting offended by me barking on him, he pulled me up and sat me in his lap like he had done many times since this whole ordeal. He rocked me back and forth like a baby as I mourned my friend. Standing up from his lap, I grabbed my phone and walked to the bathroom. I needed a sign from Mecca to let me know that everything was gonna be okay and I'd make it through the day.

Searching through our numerous text threads I found a voice note she'd left me three days before the baby shower. *"Hey, so I didn't feel like typing all this shit in text, but I just wanted you to know how very happy I am about our baby. Yes, I said our baby, Maine is gonna have to share her. You are gonna make a great mommy, Kaia, and I'm so happy to share this journey with you. I never told you this before, but I admire you so much, girl. You are the glue that keeps everything together. Like, you the Galleria to our Cheetah Girls, minus the little selfish moments. You know she was trippin' at certain times during the movie. But you, you dat bitch, boo. Now, please get ready for me to be the aunty to say yes to everything. Like no is not even gonna be in my vocabulary when it comes to my KK. And I'ma teach her how to post up on whoever try to fuck with her, too. I love you so much friend, now back to what you was talking about."*

I laughed through my tears. That was Mecca, she could make comedy out of anything, even an emotional moment. Using my shirt to wipe my tears, I looked in the mirror. *"I'm ready now, sis. And I love you, too."*

Maine came up behind me and kissed my ear while telling me how proud he was of me and to feed his baby before he whipped my ass. Grinning, I showered and got dressed in my all white as Ms. Lynn requested. Walking out into the living room, I found my family all gathered together, dressed in their all white. Amongst the crowd, I spotted Shanice at the same time her eyes met mine and we ran to each other. We fell into a tight embrace for the first time in days. We had both decided to allow the other to take their time to mourn.

"We're gonna be okay," she said to me while kissing my cheek.

"You promise?" I was always the most emotional of the group and it took me a while to process things.

"I promise, sis. She wouldn't have it any other way." I wiped my eyes before I let another tear drop.

Letting her go, I linked my arm with hers and we walked together, out to the limo. Although it was cold, the day was clear. It was a perfect day to lay my bestie to rest. The ride to the funeral home was quick. Before we knew it, we were being helped out and escorted to the front to sit amongst the rest of Mecca's family. Ms. Lynn spotted me first and surprisingly, she looked poised.

I walked over to hug her, and she squeezed me tightly before bending down and kissing my belly. "I'm so..." she cut me off with a wave of her hand.

"Don't do that, Kaia. This is not your fault, baby, and I don't want you to put that on yourself. You, Kaia, and Shanice are like sisters. I know you'd never put my baby in harm's way. I still love you the same and I'm gon' love KK just as much."

I needed to hear that more than I thought I did. Truth was, I had been blaming myself which was why I didn't want to come around in fear that others did as well. I hugged Ms. Lynn again before going to take my seat next to Shanice.

We laid my friend to rest in the best way possible. I carried out her request and sang "Real Big" with everything I had. Shanice read her eulogy along with a beautiful poem she had written. By the time she was done there wasn't a dry eye in the funeral home. When it was time to view the body, Maine had to hold me up. My legs almost gave out on me, but I kept it together. As the funeral director closed the casket, the choir sang "Missing You" by Brandy.

Though I'm missing you (although I'm missing you), I'll find a way to get through (I'll find a way to get through), living without you. Cause you were my sister, my strength, and my pride, only God may know why, still I will get by.

Ms. Lynn held onto her sister as she silently broke down. I couldn't do it anymore. Excusing myself, I went to walk outside to get some air. As I got closer to the door, I felt a gush of liquid running down my legs. With the white dress I had on, it was clear to see that my water had broken.

"Arghhh shoot, not right now, babygirl," I said before a contraction hit that almost knocked me off my feet.

"Shit Kaia, your water broke, sis," Kris said from behind me. Wrapping my arm around her neck, she called out to Maine. She was panicking, which in turn made me anxious, and that was the last thing I needed right now.

"Kristen, I need you to breathe so I can follow your lead. Right now, you're making me nervous."

"Oh okay, I'm sorry. Maine, bring yo ass cause I'm losing it, and she needs someone sane right now. Come on, I'm riding with y'all," she barked demands.

I watched as people filed out of the funeral home, and I figured the pallbearers would be bringing Mecca out next. I didn't want to miss that.

"Wait, babe. Let me see them bring her out since I won't be able to go to the burial."

"Kaia, getcho ass in that car and go deliver a healthy baby," Ms. Lynn scolded from the steps. She smiled and gave me a thumbs up.

"Yea, what she said," my mother cosigned and shooed me in the car. I got in the backseat of Maine's Bentley truck, and we drove off once Kris was in the front seat.

"Wait, did you tell Shanice what was happening?" I asked Kris.

"Yea, I'm gonna keep her posted and she's gonna meet us there." I nodded and gritted my teeth as another contraction hit.

"Oohh, motherfucka. Shit, these joints are intense, what the hell? Babe, you gotta drive fast so I can get this little girl outta me." He didn't respond, only shook his head that he understood. "Maineeee, why you not saying nothin'?"

"I'm focused, shorty. Do that breathing shit they taught you and let me get my mind right." Kris snickered and I gave her a silent, *fuck you*.

"Ouchhh, come on, we gotta get there." It took us fifteen minutes to get to my mother's hospital and only a few minutes to get me checked in. I'd gone from contracting every three to four minutes to every two minutes. Kymani was coming, and she was coming fast.

"Well alright, looks like somebody is ready to have a baby," Dr. Ross said excitedly from behind her mask. I didn't know what she was so damn happy about, wasn't no baby bout to rip her asshole. "Ok mommy, u're allowed to have two people in the room. Mom is not inc ed."

"Why my mama can't be in here?"

"Cause I'm already suited to be here, by." My mom came into view in her nurse uniform. I smile and she held my hand and kissed my forehead.

"Shitttt, it's another one. Oh God, Dr. Ross, ist get in there and get her. Kris, you and Maine stay. Oh ay God, where is Maine?" I looked around and didn't see him in sight.

"I'm right here, bae." He came wearing a pair of scrubs, with a digital camera in his hand. "I had to suit up first."

"You not about to put my coochie on video, Maine, so you might as well put that damn camera down. I'm so serious." The staff bust out laughing and Maine shook his head. I didn't give a damn, that was a memory I didn't want. The doctor checked me, and I was a full ten centimeters dilated which meant I was too far along to even think about getting the epidural. That meant I had to push without drugs, and I just didn't think the shit was fair at all.

After twelve minutes of pushing, Kymani Amor Brown made her debut at seven pounds, two ounces. When the doctor put her on my chest, I instantly thought about Mecca. I knew me giving birth on the day my best friend was laid to rest was a sign. This day would forever be a day for us to celebrate.

Kristen

Seeing my sister give birth to my niece moved me to tears. Yet and still, I had no attachment to the baby I was carrying. It had been two months since Mecca's burial and the debut of baby KK. She was so pretty with a head full of hair that always looked like she had a fresh doobie. I was in love with my little niecey pooh. While we all doted on her every chance we got, everyone had fallen back into their normal routines.

Although Kane was still in the wind, I decided to live my life and not become a hermit. What no one knew outside of Heaven, was that I had devised a plan to get to Kane through China. Of course, it sounded crazy being that she was apart

of the whole kidnapping and had taken a part in abusing me. That was a detail I hadn't forgot, I just had to put it on the back burner to think of the bigger picture. After threatening to go to the police with what they'd done to me and the possibility of her daughter going into foster care, she was on board with turning on Kane.

See, while they held me hostage, I was able to get a glimpse of how China interacted with her daughter. If the baby cried, during one of China's many assaults on me, she would stop to check on her. She loved that little girl more than life itself. The thought of being away from her scared China half to death. While she fed me information on Kane's movements, she claimed she didn't know about the shooting. I had no choice but to believe it.

The day after everything happened, I reached out to her only to be hung up on after saying *hello*. It didn't take much to figure out that it was Kane who answered. I hadn't heard from her since then. A part of me thought that he may have put two and two together. Hell, I knew he did but at this point, I was focusing on rebuilding me until I heard from her again. Starting with the grand reopening of my shop.

"This is so exciting, cousin. It looks like a whole new place. Well worth the wait, boo," Heaven complimented the turn out.

"Yes sissy, this is so nice. People bout to be lined up around the corner to get in here tomorrow," Kaia added as she rocked KK back and forth in her arms. Motherhood looked good on her.

"Yea, finally I can see all the plans right in front of me. I hope Ant can make it back in time for the opening tomorrow."

I was a little sad that Ant had been on tour with Maine and his other artists for the better part of the last month and a half. We spoke everyday but it was nothing like having his presence here. True to his word, he made sure I had around the clock security. While the detail was hired to look out for me, I also made sure to always have my own special protection as well.

"I know. Maine missed our six-week check in. All that waiting I did for nothing."

"Girl, I'm sure he was right there on FaceTime when you took the baby to see the doctor."

"I'm not talking about for KK, I'm talking about my six weeks." She pat her vagina, making Heaven giggle and me squeal.

"Eww, we didn't need to know all that now."

"I'm just saying, it's only but so much these fingers can do." I shook my head at her nasty ass. A knock on the door put a pause in our conversation. Looking through the blinds, I saw my detail, Marcus.

"Hey, everything okay?"

"Yea, there's a woman out here with a baby who's asking to speak with you." Not wanting to tip him off to my suspicion, I gave him the okay to let her in. I looked back to the girls who moved closer to the door to see who the mystery guest could have been.

"Oh unh, unh. Heaven take the baby real quick." Kaia passed the baby off to Heaven before she could respond and moved in on China who had entered with a pair of Jackie O shades covering her eyes, pushing a stroller.

"Wait, wait, Kaia." I was able to get the door closed before Marcus could have something to report back to Ant. Then China was as good as dead.

"Wait my ass, she about to get this work. Move, Kristen." Kaia tried to push pass me as I stood in front of her to calm her down. China did nothing but stand close to the exit. I whispered in Kaia's ear for her to calm down and let me talk. Letting her know I'd explain everything later, I instructed Heaven to put KK back in Kaia's arms so that she could control her hands.

"I didn't come here to start no drama. I only came with information," China spoke. I'm sure that did nothing for Kaia. All that was on my sister's mind was that *this* woman played a part in me being hurt.

"Have a seat, China," I offered.

"No bitch, stand. Bitches like you don't deserve kindness. Go head and say what you gotta say and be on your way." I cut my eyes in Kaia's direction and she shrugged her shoulders. Heaven knew what was going on, so she just stood by watching.

"I can understand the hostility and I'm not going to say I'm not deserving. Kristen, I want to apologize for what I allowed to go on as well as the part I played in kidnapping you. I've been under Kane's spell for so long that it was natural to hate you as soon as you came around. Now, I'm not placing the blame on him for my wrong doings, he has been hell times two to deal with. Having a daughter of my own and thinking of her being put in that position really put things into perspective for me." She removed her glasses and revealed two black eyes and a cut on her forehead. "I'm ready to execute the plan whenever you are."

"Damn, he been whooping yo ass," Heaven let out.

"Just like I'm bout to do," Kaia announced, putting KK back into Heaven's arms.

"Kaia, enough!"

"Enough my ass! This bitch let her so called man rape you. I'm whooping her ass!"

"Well, come—." China didn't finish her sentence before Kaia rushed her, with a quick two piece to the head, dazing her. Stepping back, allowing China to recover, Kaia took a fighter stance. She got that boxing shit honestly from hanging out with Mase and watching old Tyson fights. "Run up, bitch."

China went to charge at Kaia, but it was clear that the first two hits sent to her head, put her at a disadvantage because she was too slow. Kaia grabbed her and managed to knee her in the face. She was out for blood.

"Arghhh," China let out, falling to the floor.

"Alright, Kaia, come on." I had to pull her back because I needed China to leave in one piece if I wanted her to carry out the rest of my plan.

"You one lucky bitch, I'll tell you that," Kaia spat, snatching away from me.

China stumbled as she stood up, embarrassment was written all over her face. I didn't feel sorry for her one bit, it had taken a lot of strength to keep from pouncing on her myself, and a few talks with Heaven to keep her in line. China knew she deserved every bit of what she got. Using her baby's stroller to hold onto, she shot daggers at Kaia before leaving out.

"I don't know what you got going on, but I don't trust that bitch and you crazy as hell if you do." Kaia grabbed KK and walked to the back of the shop.

She didn't have to trust China or know about my plan. I knew what I was doing.

THE NIGHT of my grand reopening had finally come and the outpouring of love was amazing. Heaven outdid herself working with the event planner to make this night bigger and better than the first one. Outside, there was a long red carpet along with a backdrop that had the salon's name and a picture of me. Photographers snapped pictures of everyone as they entered the building dressed to the nines. I watched from the backseat of a Rolls Royce Wraith that Ant had sent to pick me and Kaia up.

With the RSVP list doubling in size almost overnight, I rented out the building next to my shop for people to mingle and eat. My goal was to make this grand reopening an experience and so far, we'd gone beyond that. I was on cloud nine and couldn't nothing stop me from smiling tonight.

"I'm so happy for you, sister. Didn't I tell you that you could do this shit...again?"

I turned to Kaia and smiled through the tears that welled up in my eyes. "Yea, you did. I'm so overwhelmed, sis. Look at all these damn people."

"I know, boo. They came out for you. Your skills got these people out here in they best shit," she giggled. "These bitches ain't fuckin' witchu, sissy. Let's go show them the hair boss is back in town." She let the driver know that we were ready, and he got out to open the door for us.

As we stepped out of the car, a blacked-out Denali truck pulled up behind us. When the doors to the truck opened, I watched as Ant stepped out of it with a smirk on his face.

"Babyyy!" I shrieked, running to him, careful not to slip in my YSL pumps. He held his arms out for me and lifted me off my feet once I was close. "Why you didn't tell me you was coming?" I playfully hit his chest and kissed his juicy lips. Ant looked so good with his dreads freshly twisted, hanging past his shoulders and a fresh line up.

Dripped in Prada and ice, his swag gave every bit of, **that nigga.**

"Then it wouldn't have been a surprise, right?" He leaned in to nuzzle my neck and squeezed my booty. "You look damn good, baby."

"Thank you, daddy." I wrapped my arms around his neck and as we inhaled each other, I felt a pair of eyes on us.

Standing behind the passenger door of the truck, wearing a noticeable frown on her face was Genesis aka Ginny B, the sultry R&B singer signed to Promise Records. I'd only met her in passing, exchanging a few pleasantries and cordial smiles. Certainly not enough interaction to really get a read on someone. However, tonight, the look in her eyes was anything but pleasant. I made a mental note to address it with Ant at a later date. Right now, I wanted to celebrate me and what better way to do that than with my man by my side.

We partied hard and didn't clear out the place until a little after two a.m. Not only were people there to celebrate, but they also took the opportunity to lock in their appointments. The shop was sure to be busy for the next two months, and I loved that for us. After ensuring that everything and everyone had cleared out, I headed home with my baby. We'd taken the next step in our relationship and officially moved in with each other about a month ago.

I had a feeling that Ant's push for me moving in had a lot to do with the Kane situation, but either way, I was fine with it. I'd been at his place more than my own since we'd been together anyway. Tonight, both KK and Bre were staying the night with his mom, so we were kid free, and I was in the mood to do tricks on the dick.

"I missed you," I spoke between kisses to his neck and face. I was in heat and couldn't keep my hands off him.

"I missed you more, ma. I'm so damn proud of what you accomplished tonight." I smiled at him gushing over me. He made sure to be there in every way, encouraging me to make changes and not take no for an answer when it came to what I envisioned for the remodel.

"Oh, yea? Show me how proud."

He unzipped my jumpsuit while placing sensual, slow kisses down my spine, making me shiver. Ant's level of intimacy took me on a high that I never knew existed. He had mastered the art of four play, taking his time stripping me naked, kissing along my calves, down to the back of my ankles.

"Bend over, spread your legs, and hold your ankles, baby. I should be able to see that pussy winking at me from the back."

Excited about what was to come, I assumed the position as requested. When I felt him spread my cheeks and swirl his tongue around my asshole, I knew I was in for a long night of intense fuckin'. My pussy knew it too because she was leaking and hadn't been touched yet. Pressing his tongue against my asshole, he continued to pleasure me while simultaneously, using his thumb to play with my clit.

"Ooouuu, baeeee, what are you doing to meeeee?" I squealed in delight, trying to stand up straight to keep from bucking at the knees.

"Unh, unh, you gon' gimmie this pussy. Bend over." **WHAP!** He smacked my ass hard, and I trembled, feeling both pain and pleasure.

"Ahhhhh, nigga that hur...oouuu, shit, eat that pussy, baby." The stinging subsided as soon as he latched onto my clit.

"Yea, shut the fuck up," he said in the middle of his tongue assault on my pussy.

"Damn, Antwon, I'ma bout to cum so hard, daddy." I slowly rocked against his tongue, feeling myself about to explode.

"Come on, gimmie that good shit."

"Ouuuu, ouuuu, I'm cummin'!" I screamed out, and my legs shook uncontrollably. It was clear that this man was trying to drain me as he sucked harder on my clit. "Baeeee, pleaseeee." I pleaded for mercy. He continued to lap at my juices until I stopped shaking.

"That pussy so juicy for me." He gave my wet mound a few kisses before allowing me to stand up.

Catching my breath, I recovered quickly and turned around. Sauntering my naked ass over to the couch, I laid back and spread my legs wide for him to see my pink flesh. "The prettiest thing you ever did see, huh."

Nodding in agreement, he stripped out of his clothes,

biting his lip, staring at me hungrily. Once his boxers hit the floor, my teeth sunk into my bottom lip. Ant had a dick on him that I found a privilege to suck, it was just that fucking perfect. Anxious, I slid to the edge of the couch, knowing he was going to place me there anyway. He smirked and kneeled down, placing one knee on the floor while steady on the other. Tapping my pussy with his dick, he slid into me, making it disappear.

"Sssssss," I hissed as he pulled it back out slowly and did the same motion again a few times until I coated his dick. Not one to be outdone, I turned so that I was on my side and guided him inside me with no hands.

"Goddamn Kris, you not playing fair," he let out as I threw my ass back.

"Ouuuu, this my dick, Antwon? Tell me this my dick." I talked and threw my ass harder at the same time.

"Shit, yea, it's yo dick. Work that shit, fuckkk, you gon' make me buss."

"You not gon' give it away, bae?"

"Nah, mmmm, it's yours, Kris." Not fully satisfied with his answer, I spread my ass cheeks and rode the dick slower.

"Mmmmm, shit, you...promise?"

"Arghhhh, I promise!" Holding onto my cheeks, he slammed into me, releasing everything he had. "Goddamn, girl, what you tryna do to me?"

"Make sure you keep lovin' me."

Leaning down with his dick still pulsating inside of me,

he kissed my lips. "You ain't gotta fuck me good to make sure I keep lovin' you, Kristen. The way you make love to a nigga's mind ensures that my heart and soul will forever be yours."

My heart fluttered and my nipples hardened. "Damn, that was deep. Come put your dick in the back of my throat so you can nut on my heart."

"Don't mind if I do."

For the rest of the night, we made love, fucked, made love, and fucked some more until we both were spent, eventually falling asleep in the living room. Couldn't nothing or no one disrupt the peaceful space that we were in.

Maine

Tour life was lit but it was nothing like being back home with my family. Although I made it my business to talk to Kaia every day, it was nothing like being in my girl's presence. She had a nigga out here love drunk, and I wasn't too gangsta to admit that. She held it down with a whole newborn in my absence and not once did she complain or make me feel bad for being on tour. Kaia encouraged my career, even going as far as to stay up some nights to motivate me while I was in the studio. Opinionated as ever, she was quick to let me know when something was corny, or a bar just didn't fit in a song. Shorty was the one forreal.

While all was well in my home, I hadn't seen my son since I dropped him off the day of the baby shower. Kandice had gon' ghost and conveniently stopped answering my calls the day after the shooting happened. At first, I thought she was just being on some spiteful shit because I hadn't picked him up the next day for obvious reasons, but when my unanswered calls went from a couple days to weeks, I knew something was up. Come to find out, her unstable ass had been in cahoots with the nigga Kane, too. I'd received a DM on IG letting me know to watch out for Kandice and that she was involved in the shooting. Yea, I could've snatched my son up, but I wanted shit done right. I knew once I went to get him, she'd never see him again.

"I gotta tell you something, shorty. And I need you to forgive me in advance for not telling you sooner." Kaia and I were laid up, coming down off an orgasmic high after two rounds of morning sex. She moved her head from my chest and sat up with a raised brow. "Why you gettin' up like you wanna throw hands?"

"I'm getting prepared just in case I don't like what I hear, and I have to punch you in yo shit, go head." She crossed her arms across her bare chest, and I fought the urge to laugh.

"I can't tell if you wanna fight a nigga or you want me to lick on them titties."

"Tremaine, stop playin' wit me."

"What? Yo nipples hard as fuck right now, look in the mirror."

"Don't worry bout my damn nipples, cause if you tell me some shit I don't like, you won't be suckin' on them no time soon. Say what you gotta say."

"Aight, man. I found out that Kandice linked up with Kane and is connected to the shooting that happened at the baby shower. I don't know how and when they linked up but yea, she down with that nigga."

"What the fuck?! Does this nigga have a stable of bitches he teams up with to do his dirty work? And wassup with y'all baby mamas?" I sat back as she got up and paced the floor while rambling. *At least she didn't punch me in my shit,* was all that I could think about. "So that's why you can't get in contact with her to see Chase? Call her private and see if she answers." She'd gone from pacing to throwing clothes on and I still had yet to move. "Why you sitting there? Call her so we can see about the baby. If she don't answer, we goin' over there. Shoot, if you would've told me sooner, I would've been at that bitch's address, the fuck."

I wasn't about to waste time calling when I knew she was gonna send me to voicemail anyway. Instead, I got up and threw my clothes on, too. I could hear Kaia talking to herself from the bathroom as I got myself together. I knew she'd want to ride being that the shooting ended in Mecca's death. She still woke up in night sweats often thinking about that night. In the car I bumped Nipsey Hussle's "Marathon" album as we drove to Kandice's mom's house.

Pulling up to the curb, I spotted Kandice's car outside. I

couldn't get a word out before Kaia was out the car and stomping into the building. I made sure my gun was tucked. I may have been on the rise with this rap shit, but the safety of my family would be ensured at all times. Once we made it up the steps, I stood behind Kaia as she knocked on the door. When no one answered immediately, she went to knock again, and I could hear the locks click. Opening the door, Kandice stood behind it. Kaia didn't let her get a word out before she rushed her.

"Bitch, you wanna play with guns," Kaia said as she punched Kandice in the side of her head, making her fall over a chair. "Get up bitch, you been wanting this for a long time. Here's your special fuckin' delivery."

She went to swing again, but Kandice ducked and tried to sweep Kaia off her feet by bear hugging her. Quickly maneuvering out of the hug, Kaia's fist connected again, only this time it was to Kandice's ribs, knocking the wind out of her. Before she could go at her again, I grabbed Kaia by her arm.

"Where's the baby, Kandice?"

"Fuck you," she spat. "Y'all deserve everything that's coming to y'all. Take ya fucking son, I didn't really want him anyway." I almost let Kaia loose when she said that shit, but she wasn't even worth it. She did all this in hopes that I would be with her.

"You went and got yourself acquainted with a nigga that beat his bitches for blinking. And now you're a target in these streets. This shit between you and me ain't over. We lost a family member behind that shooting. Congratulations, you played yourself."

Kaia reappeared with Chase on her hip and we walked out the same way we came in. Strapping him in KK's seat, we pulled off and headed back home. While driving, I put in a call to have Kandice handled. I didn't trust that she wouldn't have me arrested for kidnapping or some other off the wall shit. Unlike Ant, a bitch wasn't gon' be able to play in my face twice.

OVER THE NEXT FEW DAYS, I played the crib with my family, and it was an adventure to say the least. Kaia fell right into the mommy role with Chase and didn't skip a beat with KK. My daughter was the shit. She had her mommy's complexion but everything else was all me. I guess that would be accurate being that Kaia couldn't stand my ass for a while during the pregnancy. I had gotten past the Kandice issue, but now I had another problem on my hands. One that was created while I was out on tour.

Like I said before, tour life had been good to me thus far and in a couple days, I would be going back out on the road. I didn't count on having an issue with one of the artists, but here I was. I may have given the new artist, Ginny B, the wrong impression about this thing called friendship by just tryna be a decent person. The first night of our tour, I found her crying backstage and yelling at someone over the phone. Everyone seemed to go about their business as if they didn't see the distraught female. I really blamed Kaia for activating the caring side of a nigga.

"Yo, you need a minute? You're up after Boog. Take a minute and come back." She nodded and ran off.

Once Boog's set was done, I watched her go out and command the stage as if she wasn't losing it a few moments before. That night, we went out to celebrate our first successful show and she pulled me to the side.

"Thank you for helping me get it together. I'm embarrassed that you even had to see me that way."

"You good. I hope everything is straight on your end. You did ya thang tonight on stage."

She smiled and shrugged her shoulders. "I do a little sum'n, sum'n. It's nothing compared to how you go up there and rock the crowd though."

From that day on, we became cool. Well, as cool as cool could get without Kaia looking at me sideways if she found out. While waiting on Kaia to hook up a quick dinner, I laid on the couch watching tv, with both Chase and KK sleeping in their playpen. My phone chimed and a text from Ginny popped up.

Ginny B: *Hey, I'm at the studio and Playboy just played this dope beat that I can hear us on. You mind coming through and blessing the track real quick?*

Me: *Oh word? That's wassup. I gotta pass though, my lady* *is cooking dinner and I wanna spend the next few days with the family ya know.*

Ginny B: yea, I get it. Wish I had a man that wanted to be up under me as much as you want to be under your woman. She is a lucky girl for sure. I'd trade places with her in a heartbeat. Anyway, let me get back to creating this magic. You have a good night, Maine.

I read the text and quickly shook off her flirting before deleting the whole thread. She had been doing that a lot lately. Texting me randomly, either wanting me to come to the studio or just to see what I was doing. I had made the mistake of giving her my number one night, again, on some friendly shit. Now my friendly ass was dealing with some high school crush type shit.

"Babe, you want me to bring ya food out there?" Kaia called out from the kitchen.

"Yea, the kids are still sleeping. I wanna be close in case they wake up." She had the house smelling right. I requested garlic chicken alfredo with the cheddar bay biscuits from Red Lobster. Bringing my food out on a tray with a glass of Kool-Aid, she sat next to me, and I dug in.

"You not eating?"

"Unh unh, I ate while I cooked. Enjoy." She kissed my forehead and grabbed the remote to flick through the channels. "Baby, your birthday is in two months, what you wanna do?"

"Nothing really. I just wanna spend time with you and

the kids. I do enough mingling and partying on tour when we host events. When I'm home, I wanna chill."

"I get that. Maybe I can come to one of the cities you're in and watch you perform. I'll be ya groupie, baby, cause you are my superstar." She sang to me and laughed.

"Them groupies out there ready to risk it all, shorty. You sure that's your speed?"

"Anything that has to do with you is my speed." Winking, she stuck her tongue out and rubbed my dick through my sweats.

"You tryna see bout a nigga?" Nodding, she stood and pulled her house dress over her head, revealing the perfect naked body, complete with the postpartum tummy that she was insecure about. I made sure to kiss it every night so that she knew there wasn't a part on her body that I didn't love.

Checking on the babies once more to make sure they were sound asleep, I gave her the thumbs up. Pulling my boxers and sweats down to my ankles, I sat back while she climbed in my lap. Planting both feet on either side of me, she slid down on my dick slowly.

"God, yess," she crooned. It didn't make no sense how her pussy stayed biting at my dick when I hit her. "Yesss baby, just like that," she encouraged, burying her face in my neck as I spread her ass cheeks and hit her with medium strokes.

She knew my neck and my balls were sensitive spots for me. Sinking her teeth in my neck, she clenched her pussy muscles at the same time. That little move made me drill her harder until I felt her pussy leaking. As she came, I licked along her collar bone, moving my hips in a circular motion as I slow stroked her. Feeling my nut build up, I held her down and emptied my seeds in her womb.

"Ughhhh, shittt. Damn, you keep fucking me like that and it's gon' be some more kids running round here."

Kissing my lips, she hopped up and switched off to the bathroom. Getting up to put on my boxers, I picked up my phone to check the time, and I had another text from Ginny.

Ginny B: *Wow, you are quite the lover. Again, she's a lucky girl. I wish I could've seen the show up close.*

My brow raised, clueless as to what she was talking about. It soon became clear once I checked my call log to see that I had called her while Kaia and I were having sex. Her crazy ass had sat and listened the whole time. More problems I didn't need.

Ant

Things were looking up for the kidd in a major way. We were on the last leg of the tour and the bag had been secured. I was so fuckin' proud of my team. Tonight was the last performance, and it was being held in our city at the Barclays Center. Seeing all the family gathered backstage for support was dope. It would be the first time they saw Maine live on a big stage, so they were in for a surprise as well as the audience. Maine and Ginny B had just finished a track together that they were going to premiere it to close out the show.

"Ay, can I have everybody's attention? Grab a glass of

champagne, I wanna make a quick toast." Everyone went to grab a glass, including Kris. I gave her a look and she sucked her teeth before putting it back down. Her five-month-old belly was round and on display. That was about the only thing that changed when it came to the pregnancy, her attitude remained the same. "I wanna thank all of you for making this tour the first of many successful tours to come. To the artists, y'all some dope ass people man. I couldn't have picked a better squad. To the family, thank you for holding down the home front and making it possible for us to do what we do."

After my little speech, everyone raised their glasses in a toast to success. I scanned the room, taking in all my people in attendance, and my eyes stopped at Ginny B. She was a real cool girl. Sometimes I would catch her drifting off like she was in deep thought, but overall, she was cool. A real beast at her craft, too. Her aura seemed off tonight, though. Her face struggled to maintain the smile that she was forcing and as I followed her line of sight, it landed on Maine and Kaia who were off in the corner engrossed in each other.

"Wassup Ginny, you ready to premiere the song tonight?" Clearly distracted, her head turned quickly in my direction.

"He...hey, yeah, I'm ready," she stuttered.

"Aight, well, have a drink. You seem preoccupied and I want you to go out and give this performance your all."

"You got it, boss," she said with a smile before walking

away awkwardly. I watched Kris watch Ginny before coming toward me. Her stride was alarming, and she was sporting a mug.

"Wassup with her?"

"What you mean?"

"I mean, why she look like she lost her best friend when she's looking at Maine and Kaia? At first, I thought she had something for you, but after watching her tonight, it's clear to see that she wants Maine." I didn't confirm or deny. "Dammit, Antwon," she slapped my arm. "Your face alone says you knew, or you had a feeling something was there."

"I don't know or feel nothing and I'm not getting in between that."

"Yeah okay, she's gonna be a problem. I can already see it. And since you wanna act clueless, keep that same energy when you wanna be inside me tonight. Coochieville is closed until further notice, sir." She left me standing there and all I could do was say a silent prayer that this didn't come back to bite me in the ass. Right now, we had a show to do.

After each artist performed their individual hits, the lights went down on stage except for a spotlight off to the side. Ginny stood in that spotlight in a two-piece short set that was covered in Swarovski crystals. Her look screamed sex symbol.

"Brooklyn! Y'all read for a treat tonight?" She yelled out into the crowd, making them go wild with applause. "That's what I like to hear. I wanna play my new record for y'all, it's called, "Four Play". Can I make it just a little nasty for my fellas tonight?" You could hear the guys in the crowd making howling noises. "Don't worry ladies, I got something for y'all, too. DJ, let's do this." The beat dropped and Ginny went in.

You wanna four play, you wanna gimmie a taste. You wanna four play, come put ya hands on my waist. You wanna four play, boy, ain't no stopping, why wait? You want this four play, I'll do it all day.

The chorus was catchy and had the crowd rocking. When Maine swaggered down the aisle spitting his verse, the ladies went crazy. Between the two there was so much chemistry on stage, one would think they were together. As the crowd cheered them on, Ginny turned it up a notch and dropped down in front of Maine, moving her body like a snake as she picked it back up. I didn't expect that, nor did I see the move when they had rehearsed earlier in the day.

"Ant, what the hell was that?" Kaia questioned from behind me.

"It's just for the performance, sis. You see the crowd is loving that shit." I pointed out just as I turned around to see Ginny grab Maine's face and sensually kiss him on his cheek like she wished it was his lips.

"Hmph, yeah aight."

The performance lasted all of six minutes and once they were done, the crowd was screaming for an encore. Coming off the stage, Maine appeared aggravated while Ginny was still on a high. I gathered the team so that we could all leave through the back door to avoid the crowd. I made sure security covered us as we exited. Somehow, fans got wind of our exit plan and bombarded us at the door.

"Maine, Maine, can you sign this for me?" The women shouted from different directions, vying for bro's attention. As always, he tried to sign every paper, arm, and CD. Standing off to the side, I looked on proud. Through the crowd, I spotted a familiar face and without thinking, I pulled my gun.

"Motherfucka," I gritted after seeing Kane amongst the crowd.

"What the hell are you doing?" Kris whispered harshly in my ear while grabbing my arm.

"Kane is here," I said while pulling away from her.

"So, what you gon' do? Shoot him in front of all these people, Antwon? Think, babe." Pissed to admit it, she was right. Still, I didn't want him to get away. I put my gun back up and by the time I looked back into the crowd he was gone. This nigga was getting bolder and bolder by the minute. Loading up the Sprinter we all were transported in, I sat back in deep thought. My phone chimed and there was a message from a nine two nine area code. It looked like a text free number.

929-645-2550: *She's glowing, I'm sure I have something to do with that. Do you think the baby will look like me or her?*

The picture attached was from tonight at the concert. It

was Kris's side profile as she stood outside next to me. I gripped my phone in my hand before setting it next to me. Again, he'd gotten too close. This time someone in my camp was responsible.

Kaia

I was all for Maine's success and him living out his dream. I loved to see my man on stage doing his thing, commanding the crowd. While all of that was great, the performance two nights ago with Ginny B, I could not get jiggy with. Watching her dip it low and pick it up slow in front of him was not my idea of a good time. I had to let the two days pass before I approached the situation like an adult. Trust me, I wanted to turn shit up at the concert, but I was too classy for that.

"Okay, so what should I say?" I asked Shanice who I was on the phone with while making Maine some lunch.

"**Just tell him that the performance made you feel a way. Homegirl was inappropriate,**" she stated simply.

"**Or I can handle it like Mecca would.**" We both laughed just thinking about our crazy girl.

"**Bitch, she would've gone on stage like she was a part of the damn show. Straight cuttin' the fuck up.**" I couldn't stop laughing because she told no lies. "I miss her so much."

"**Me too girl, me too.**" The phone went silent. I felt Mecca's spirit was in the room, saying she missed us, too.

We spoke a little longer and made plans for me to bring the kids over to see her. I had been back and forth between my house and Maine's loft, but mainly with him. Chase was officially apart of the household, and I was managing two kids daily. I hadn't heard anything about Kandice after I beat her ass, and I didn't ask any questions. I treated Chase the same as KK. In my eyes, he was just as much mine as he was Maine's.

"Babe," I called out to Maine who was in KK's room putting the kids down for a nap.

"You wake them up if you want to and you gon' be right in there with them."

I giggled as he turned the corner. They'd given him a run for his money with nap time today. Now he knew how I felt when I was alone. Thank God for my parents and Ma Jane who helped as often as they could.

"Boy bye, you gon' be right back in there since you don't stick to my schedule when your home. You wanna be Mr.

Fun, so deal with the consequences. Here, I made you a sandwich." He needed to be nice and full before I said what I had to say.

"Wassup?" Making himself comfortable on the couch, he sat the plate down on the coffee table.

"Why you say it like that?"

He chuckled. "You got something on your mind. I can tell by the crease in yo forehead." I stood in front of him and smiled.

"You know me so well. So, your performance the other night, I wasn't feeling the whole touchy-feely thing. Ms. Ginny really did the most. Dancing on you for entertainment is one thing, but that whole kissing ya cheek shit was a no no."

"I spoke to her about that."

"Oh, did you?"

"Yea. I told her she was out of pocket and going forward to be mindful of what she does on stage, especially with me."

"Okay, cool." That's all I wanted, and I could only give the benefit of the doubt from here. Picking up my phone, I went to the bedroom to take a nap myself. During my nap, I had the craziest dream that I walked in on Maine and Ginny having sex, in a dressing room, backstage at one of their concerts.

Oh, hell no, I'm gon' address this hoe myself.

Using my sister as the buffer, I had her set up a lunch date for the following day with Ginny and me. My goal was to make some things clear and end on a peaceful note. Should the meeting go left, I was fine with that as well.

"So, where you gonna tell Maine you going?" Kris asked over the phone as I got dressed for the meeting.

"Lunch with Shanice." Wanting to be cute but comfy, I threw on a pair of cargo joggers, a thrasher shirt, a Moto jacket, and my Loui platform boots.

Maine didn't give me any issues when I told him I was going out. He knew that a break was needed and encouraged the outing. I was sure that if he knew what I was really doing, he would've been pissed and told me to sit my ass down. But he didn't know and I wanted to keep it that way.

"Alright, call me if you need me. And keep a level head, Kaia. You can't go in there beating the girl up."

"Yea, well, let's hope it doesn't come to that. I'll call you when I'm leaving. Love you."

I chose La Bernardin as the meet up spot and reserved a table for us in the back. In the back of the black Escalade, I thought of all the ways the conversation could go left but remained optimistic. Five minutes after I arrived and had been seated, Ginny walked in dressed to the nines in a leather pencil skirt, a silk shirt, and a peacoat that rested on her shoulders. Her Giuseppe heels hit the floor with purpose. She smiled before pulling out a chair to sit down.

"I was surprised to receive a call that you wanted to meet

with me today. I don't know whether to be worried or open to what you may have to talk to me about." Her whole aura was faker than a three-dollar bill and I was not impressed.

"Well, thank you for coming. Would you like to order first then talk or both?"

"Both is fine. I'm very good at multi-tasking. Do you mind if my security sits two tables down from us? You can never be too careful at this level of celebrity. I'm sure you go through it with Maine all the time."

"Already covered, but if you feel more comfortable with your people that's totally fine with me." I watched as she signaled for her security. "So, I invited you here to discuss your recent performance with Maine. Now, while I understand that certain things are done for entertainment and to capture the audience, there are some things that cross the line." As I spoke, I watched her body shift from relaxed to guarded. "You grinding on my man and kissing him is overstepping. It's obvious that you're attracted to him and that's fine, but there is a line that cannot be crossed moving forward."

What she didn't know was, I peeped game all the way back to Kris's grand reopening. I watched her intently stare me and Maine down while we were hugged up. It wasn't a stare of admiration, but more of seething *jealousy*. I was very observant, especially when it came to my man, my family, and my money. And not necessarily in that order.

"Oh," she said, reaching for her water. Putting the glass to her lips, she watched me over the rim as she took a slow sip and placed it back on the table. "Please forgive me if I made you feel threatened in any way. Make no mistake about it, everything I did that night was to please the crowd only. I mean a blind woman can see that Maine is attractive, but again my actions are solely to entice the crowd." She put her hand on her chest apologetically and I was just about over the fake shit.

"I may not have made myself clear in my statement." I sat up so that she could not only hear but *feel* what I was about to say. "Ain't a woman alive that can make me feel threatened. That man that you perform with comes home to me nightly and doesn't miss a beat when it comes to knocking my pussy out the frame and eatin' a bitch up like a fruit roll up. And yes, he is very attractive, I can agree with you there. My thing is to ensure that women such as yourself admire his looks, swag, etc. from afar. Anything I deem out of line will be addressed."

"Noted."

"I'm glad we had this conversation. You enjoy your lunch, it's covered." I didn't actually plan on breaking bread with her. I put my order in to go unbeknownst to her. The waitress walked out with a bag for me, and a plate was placed in front of her. Putting my jacket back on, I showed her how a real bad bitch pushed through. My ass didn't hit the seat in the car fully before my phone rang.

"Yes, babe?" I answered putting the phone on speaker, already knowing it was Maine calling.

"You know you crazy, right?" I could hear the smile in his voice.

"Why? What I do?"

"Why you went and met with that girl when I already told you I spoke to her?"

Oh, what a snitch ass bitch, I chuckled to myself. "Paul, can you ride back around to the restaurant so I can go kick Ginny B's ass?"

"Paul, you know Joann ain't gon' wanna hear shit you gotta say if you go home jobless," Maine threatened.

Paul looked at me and laughed. I mouthed, *I got you* to him and he shook his head.

"Don't threaten my security. I'm on my way back." I hung up the phone and threw it in my purse next to me. I had accomplished what I set out to do, now it was up to Ginny to take heed of the warning.

Kane

"Damn, she told you," I clowned as I slid in the chair that Kaia once occupied. The buff looking bouncer Ginny had with her stood to walk over to me and she waved him off with her hand.

"What the hell are you doing here, Kane?" She spoke through the fake smile she had plastered on her face. I had my hoodie halfway covering my head so that I wouldn't scare anyone off.

"I told you I'd be stopping by to see you soon. And here I am." I reached over and plucked a fry from her plate and ate it. "Looks like you were having a deep conversation with Maine's woman. It wouldn't have anything to do with that hot performance, now would it?" I had attended the concert, and I must say, I didn't see what all the hype was about. It was a good thing that I didn't have to pay for a ticket. It was free, courtesy of my little cousin, the R&B sensation, Ginny B.

"That is none of your business and we both agreed that if we ever needed to meet, it would be at my place."

"My dear little cousin, you are my business. I'll meet you at your condo, the key still under the mat?" She let out a frustrated sigh before replying *yes*. Getting up, I stole another fry and made my way to the exit.

I knew she was over me, but we were just getting started. Ginny and I were first cousins. Her mother was my aunt on my dad's side. Growing up, we were around each other all the time because her mom had a bad drug habit and often left her with our grandmother. I was there a lot, too, being that my dad was always working. Throughout the years, we had become estranged, mainly due to her going over to the opposite side of the tracks. Every now and then I'd reach out to check in just to make sure she was doing okay.

The last time we were in contact before now was last year. She needed my help getting a sex tape her ex-boyfriend/pimp was threatening to leak of her. Using my status, I was successful in getting the tape back. Now, she owed me and even family had to pay.

"You're a little too comfortable. Get out of my fridge, Kane!" She barked, entering her condo as I helped myself to a fruit bowl she had in the fridge.

"You need to work on your hospitality, woman."

"No, you need to tell me what you want so you can get the fuck out. Are you trying to get me killed?" She slammed her phone and bag on the table.

"Please refrain from using that tone with me. I wouldn't have to pop up on you if you answered my calls and texts." I closed the fridge and popped a grape in my mouth.

"In case you forgot, I'm an entertainer and I have a busy schedule to keep to. I can't always be at your beck and call." She really had let stardom go to her head and she wasn't even half as big as that Dream Doll chick off *Love & Hip Hop* to me. Getting in her face, I had to remind her of where she came from.

"How quickly we forget that you're the same person who was turning tricks just a year ago. You were singing on a different mic then. You owe me and it's best that you stop forgetting that, cousin." She took a step back to create space between us.

"I don't wanna keep doing this, Kane. If they find out, my career and possibly my life could be over."

I could see her going soft on me and I couldn't have that. Initially, the plan was for her to get close to Ant and seduce him into having sex with her. I knew Kris wouldn't tolerate a cheater. So far, she failed at that because Ant wouldn't bite. Ant was all about the business and kept it strictly about the music. Maine was the next best thing and she had gotten a little further with him, but I needed her to step it up a notch.

"You don't wanna keep doing this because of your career or are you falling for him?" Silence. I knew the answer already and this would work to my advantage. "Listen, you need to get him alone and vulnerable. Right now, you're being too passive, I need you to get aggressive and fast. Remember, your career depends on it." Dropping her key on the table in front of her, I left out.

Now that my arm had healed about eighty-five percent, I was back to moving around by myself. The night of the concert, I tried to blend in with the crowd as best I could but was easily spotted by Ant. That was my fault, though. I let my emotions get the best of me when I saw Kristen's round stomach. My heart two-stepped in my chest after realizing it was a baby bump. There was no doubt in my mind that the baby was mine.

I made sure to line her womb with my seeds each time I was inside of her. I'm sure she'd want to curl up and die once she found out that I knew. After the babies of mine she had killed, I thought she wouldn't be able to carry in the future. This was our miracle baby. That only made me want to go harder to get her back. There was no way I would allow her to raise my kid with Ant. I envisioned us being a little family. Only our family would be unorthodox because it would include China, Kristine, and Chloe.

I hadn't heard from Kandice in a while, and I needed to know how she was holding up since the shooting. It was a fact that loose lips sunk ships and I couldn't be the one on the drowning end. Taking out my phone, I sent her a text that she needed to reach out to me asap. Entering my house, I overheard China talking on the phone, catching the tail end of the conversation.

"I'll call you when I'm on my way," she said before hanging up and turning around, bumping right into me.

"On your way where?" I asked. "And where is Kristine?"

"She's with my mother and I'm on my way out to meet up with a friend." She tried to walk pass me, but I grabbed her back by her arm.

"Give me your phone."

"What?"

"Give...me...your...phone," I demanded sinisterly.

"I'm not giving you my phone, Kane. What is your problem? Let my arm go." She snatched away from me, and my reflexes caused me to smack her to the ground. **WHAP!** "Owww," she howled, her phone falling to the side of her. Quickly picking it up, I unlocked it and went to the last call in her call log. The phone rang twice before going to voicemail. Why would the person on the other end send her to voicemail if she was just speaking to them?

Just as I went to text the number, she lunged at me, scratching at my face. Thinking that she was fighting me because she was hiding something, I blacked out and pounced on her. I rained blow after blow on her head as she begged me to stop. Even after she was on the floor again, I didn't stop until I got tired, and she wasn't moving.

"Get ya sneaky ass up and get in the room," I demanded, winded. "Shit." My arm ached from the pressure I had put on it. "I said get up, China." I kicked at her feet, but there was no movement from her. Suddenly, I panicked. Bending down to check her pulse, there was none. "Oh shit, what the fuck?!"

The reality of what I'd just done hit me like a ton of bricks. I had just beaten China to death. The one woman who loved me in spite of me. My heart became heavy with regret. I didn't wanna kill her, she made me do it. Panicked, I called the first person that came to my mind to help me out of this shit. It was an added favor, but she would have no choice but to help me. "Ginny, I need you to get to my apartment asap. Find a way to shake your security." Things had suddenly taken a turn for the worst.

Kristen

I was nearing the end of my pregnancy and the closer I got to my due date, the more depressed I became. The only thing that gave me joy now a days was Bre and doing hair. Oh, food and a good dick down from Ant would get me up and running as well. Other than that, I was as mean as a rattlesnake.

"Babe," Ant called my name and I played sleep. I heard him laugh as he walked in the room. Yanking the covers off my head, he slapped my thigh. "I know you not sleep. I just left the room not even ten minutes ago."

"Ughh, what you want? I just wanna sleep. This baby

done absorbed all my energy. I don't even feel like getting up to go to the bathroom," I whined.

"That's not an option because if you fuck around and piss on these thousand thread count sheets, we gon' have a problem, love."

"Yea whatever, what you want?"

"I need you to get up. I got a surprise for you." I gave him an evil eye and that he ignored. Pulling at my arms, he forced me out of bed.

"Ughh, you aggravating today, huh."

He laughed and held a blind fold up to my face. "Put this on and I'm not taking no for an answer." I obliged but not without a stomp of my feet and swing of my arms. The only thing that made me perk up a little was the smell of food as he held my hand and led me down the stairs.

"Damn, it smells good as hell in here. Did my mom drop by and bring her honey bbq ribs?" As we reached the last steps the smell became more potent.

"Alright, now you can take it off." Pulling off the blindfold I heard, SURPRISE! And was speechless seeing the living room decorated with a bunch of baby stuff. Our immediate family stood underneath a congratulations banner in the foyer. My eyes darted around the room before landing on Bre who had on a t-shirt that read, "I'm The Big Sister."

Turning back around, I went right back up the stairs. I heard everyone calling my name, but they were drowned out by my own thoughts. I told Ant I didn't want a baby shower. And I could count on my fingers and toes how much I said I didn't want the baby. Walking as fast as my belly would allow, I retreated to my bedroom and slammed the door behind me.

Not even a minute later, Ant was storming in behind me. "Yo, what the fuck was that?"

"What the fuck was what?" I responded nonchalantly.

"You just run out on everybody like that? They set all that up for you, Kristen. Come on now, you can't be that selfish." He had some fucking nerve calling me selfish.

"Selfish? This is coming from the man whose making me have a baby that I don't fucking want. I told you months ago that I didn't want a baby shower or celebration and you go behind my back and do it anyway. How did you expect me to react?"

"I expected you to be a fucking adult and at least be appreciative that our family wanted to do this for you because they noticed how down you've been. Everything can't *always* just be about you, Kris. There are other feelings involved here, too." After saying his peace, he left me on stuck. I felt myself about to cry and before I could catch the tear, it had already fallen.

"Knock Knock, you mind if we come in?" My mom, Kaia, and Ma Jane entered after I gave the okay.

"You sure are a mean something these days, girl," Ma

Jane said, making Kaia laugh and my mother glare at me. I could tell my mom wasn't a fan of my behavior lately, but no one could tell me how I should feel when it came to this pregnancy.

"I know and I'm sorry for the way I reacted. I just really can't celebrate wholeheartedly. This is why I specifically asked Ant not to do this." Seemingly not receptive to my response, my mother let me have it.

"Now that you were able to say your peace, let me say mine. We all understand how you feel, and we aren't faulting you for that baby. The issue is the fact that you're taking it out on the ones who love you, especially Antwon. He wanted to do something nice for you and the way you reacted was not cool." I put my head down, feeling like I was being reprimanded. She lifted my head and pointed to my stomach. "No matter whose baby you're carrying, we are going to give that baby all the love in the world. I need you to pull it together and come celebrate."

"Yea, what she said," Kaia chimed in. We all shared in a laugh as I wiped my face. She was right... about how I reacted anyway.

Dragging myself from the bed, I changed out of my house dress and threw on something more suitable for the occasion. Downstairs, the party was in full swing. I gave everyone a proper greeting and went to find Antwon so that I could apologize. Finding him in the kitchen talking to Maine, and my dad. I hugged him from behind. Maine smirked and made his exit. My dad went to follow behind him and stopped next to me.

"Stop giving the man a hard time, princess. Don't let what happened turn you cold. We got you, most importantly, he got you." With a quick peck to my forehead, he left.

Ant didn't respond to me right away, he just stood still with his back still facing me. I sighed and as I went to unwrap my arms from around him, the baby kicked.

"Damn, karate kid, chill out," he joked, and I caught myself smiling. Now facing me, he spoke to my belly. "I know mommy been acting grumpy lately, but don't worry, once you get here, she'll be a little nicer."

"I'm sorry about how I reacted earlier and thank you for all that you do day in and day out to keep my spirits up. I love you." I kissed his lips and went to rejoin the party.

I couldn't front, I had a nice time celebrating with my family. We played a bunch of games and like a good sport, I opened all the gifts that they bought. It was around eight o' clock when everyone started to file out and I was glad for that because I sure was tired.

While Ant packed away the last of the gifts, Bre climbed in bed with me as she did often. Scooting down close to my belly, she kissed it and began talking. Tears pooled in the corners of my eyes as she talked about how she was gonna be the baby's best friend and how she couldn't wait until he or she got here. I chuckled when she mentioned her being the boss because she was the big sister. It was the cutest thing ever. The fact that Bre could be so accepting and excited about the baby and I couldn't even bear the thought of carrying it fucked me up.

All throughout the night I tossed and turned and couldn't seem to get comfortable as I slept. I looked over at Ant who slept peacefully, with one hand across his chest and the other behind his head. Not wanting to wake him, I got up and headed for the kitchen to heat up leftovers from earlier. Not being able to sleep with all this belly had become a common thing within the last couple months. On top of my belly being huge, I was also experiencing the most intense heartburn in the world. I had a month and a half to go and this whole pregnancy nightmare would be over.

Putting my food in the microwave to heat up, I poured myself a glass of milk. I couldn't get it to my lips before a pain in my stomach hit me so vicious, the glass slipped from my hand, causing it to shatter. I gripped my stomach, knowing exactly what the pains were. It was far from the baby's arrival time though. I went to call out for Ant, but another contraction ripped through me, making me hunch over.

"Antwonyyy!" I cried out. The contractions were now moving to my back and I swore I wanted to die. "Antwonyy!" I called out again.

"Kris, you okay?" I looked up just in time to see Bre

walking towards me with a face of confusion mixed with sadness.

"Wait Bre, there's glass in here, baby. You can't... mmmm..." I was cut off by another contraction and tried my best to breathe through it. "You can't walk in here, mamas. Go get daddy for me please. Tell him it's an emergency." I could kick Antwon's ass right now for being a hard sleeper. She ran off to do as I asked.

Trying to navigate around the glass and milk on the floor, I coached myself to the living room but could only make it to the dining room before another contraction crept up on me. I bit down hard on my lip, not wanting to scream out loud again. The last thing I wanted to do was scare Bre more than she already seemed to be.

"Babe, what's going on?" Ant asked, his voice filled with concern as he descended the steps.

"The baby, Ant. The baby is coming right now. We don't have time to pack or nothing. We need to go now!" Immediately, he sprang into action like super dad. Grabbing his keys and Bre, who was still in her pajamas, he threw her on his back and helped me to the door. "Wait, wait bae, you gotta go put some clothes on." He looked down at himself and shook his head. If I wasn't in so much pain, I would've been cracking up.

Racing back upstairs with Bre, he was back down in under two minutes. I knew because I'd been timing the contractions that were continuing to kick my ass. Grabbing my hand, he kissed the back of it and looked up at me.

"Let's go have a baby."

GOD MUST'VE HEARD my prayers because we made it to the hospital safely. With the way Ant was speeding, we were liable to either be stopped by police or by another car smacking us off the road. It took no time to get me checked in and into a room. Immediately, I requested an epidural for the pain.

"Okay Kristen, although you're a month shy of your due date, this baby is ready to make her debut. Are you ready to do this?" I nodded at Dr. Ross and wiped the tears that had begun to fall.

"Don't worry, I got you, baby," Ant assured me and kissed my head. "I'ma go get suited up and take Bre to the waiting area with your mom." I nodded again, even though I didn't want him to leave my sight. It took another two hours for me to get to a full ten centimeters dilated and I was ready to push.

"Come on Kristen, give me a good push," the doctor coached. I took a deep breath and pushed with all I had. "That's good, that's good, come on, again."

Again, I pushed, and we went at the same routine until

the baby was out of me. I didn't hear the normal claps and celebration that I'd seen on the birthing shows I watched from time to time or during Kaia's delivery. All I could hear were the nurses rushing around as the doctor placed the baby in an incubator.

"Why the baby not crying?"

"Everything's okay, we just have to take her down to the NICU to check her out."

"That still doesn't answer my question as to why she's not crying!" Immediately, my motherly instinct that I swore I wasn't going to have kicked in at the thought of something being wrong with my baby.

"I'll have more information for you in a moment, Kristen. Right now, let me get the baby downstairs so that I can run some tests." She rushed out of the room.

"Tests? What fucking tests?!" Ant questioned, at my side.

"Antwon, what did she look like? What's going on?" The tears in his eyes were scaring me and the unknown had me on edge.

"The cord was wrapped around her neck when she came out, bae. There was discoloration in her skin... she... she wasn't breathing."

"No, she was breathing, she *had* to have been breathing, Antwon. Please, don't say that. I swear I didn't mean what I said when I said I didn't want her!" I grabbed at his shirt, and he tried his best to hold onto me as I wailed.

"It's okay, she's a fighter, I know she is. It's okay, baby." He didn't know that for sure. He didn't know if she was okay.

We waited a few grueling hours before the doctor came back to tell us that the baby was doing okay. For the first time since she was rushed out of the room, I was able to breathe easy. Due to her small size, we were told that she would need to spend some time in the NICU, but according to the doctor, she was a fighter just like her daddy said. I listened intently as Dr. Ross went over the plan for the baby's stay and what we had to look forward to taking care of a preemie. As we were wrapping up, an alarm went off, making the doctor alert. Through the window, I could see other doctors and nurses sprinting into different areas. Something big was going on. Just as I was about to ask one of the nurses peeked in.

"Dr. Ross, we have a Code Purple. We need you in the NICU immediately," the person said in a panic-stricken voice.

"Wait, what the hell is a Code Purple?" Ant questioned before I could get the words out.

"Missing child," she responded before running out.

To Be Continued...

Did you enjoy the read?
Let us know how much by leaving us a review on Amazon
and Goodreads.

Keep reading for a preview of...

The State's Witness

By Kyiris Ashley

CHAPTER 1

Russell laid back in bed with his legs spread as he looked up at the ceiling. Tianna sat between them with his manhood in her mouth. However, she was taking way too long to make him nut. She didn't know how to suck dick at all, and he knew he would have to give her several lessons before she would be decent at it. In all of his twenty-eight years of life, he'd never had to teach a woman how to suck dick, but for Tianna, he would do so. He liked her vibe and wanted to keep her around. Russell focused his dark brown eyes on the porn that was being played on the fifty-five-inch television in front of him. He bit his bottom lip as he watched the thick, brown skinned woman get pounded from behind. Closing his eyes, he focused on the woman's moans and his dick hardened. Placing his hand on the back of Tianna's head, he pushed it down, causing his dick to go deeper down her throat.

Tianna gagged, forcing more saliva to enter her mouth. Russell grabbed one of her nipples and twirled it between his fingers as he held her head in place. With his eyes still closed, Russell's toes curled as he sensed the feeling of his climax nearing.

"Yes bitch, suck that dick for daddy. Get all that nut outta there," Russell panted, just as he released his warm cum down Tianna's throat.

Tianna sat up and wiped her mouth with her hand. She looked at the way Russell was laid out and breathing heavy, and a smile crossed her face.

"Did I do good, baby?" She asked, eager to hear his answer.

Russell had told her on several occasions that she didn't know how to perform oral sex. She knew that was something Russell really liked, and in order to keep him happy, she wanted to learn the ends and outs. So, she watched porn and searched Goggle in an effort to master the skill of giving head.

"Yeah, that was pretty dope. I'm glad no teeth came out this time. You still have some work to do but you are getting' better," Russell replied.

In reality, Russell wouldn't have came if it wasn't for the porn. He just didn't want to hurt Tianna's pride. He could tell that she really wanted to please him, so he just let her think she had done so.

"I'm gonna get in the shower, I have to work in the mornin'. Are you spendin' the night tonight?" Tianna asked as she stood from the bed.

"Nah, not to night, my baby."

Russell saw the change in Tianna's demeanor and knew she wanted him to stay, but he had money to collect. It was always money over bitches in his eyes. Tianna wasn't making him any money, so he wasn't about to keep wasting his time with her.

"How much you makin' at that little job you got?" Russell asked as he zipped his pants.

"Bout seven hundred every two weeks," Tianna answered confidently.

"What if I tell you I know a way you can double that in just one week, maybe even a few days, dependin' on how good you work?"

"I'm listenin'," Tianna replied.

"You gotta use what you got to get what you want. Has anybody ever told you that as long as you got a pussy, you should never be broke?"

Tianna looked at Russell perplexed. Did this dude just call me broke? I had just swallowed his kids while he moaned like a little bitch, and he has the nerve to stand here and insult me? I may not be big ballin', but I was definitely livin' comfortably. Tianna thought, quickly becoming irritated by the way Russell was talking to her.

"No disrespect, my baby, I'm just tryin' to put you up on game. Let's be real, you been fuckin' and suckin' on me for the last six weeks, for free. I'm sure it's a dozen other niggas that can say that too."

"Are you suggesting that I should fuck for money?" Tianna asked, damn near ready to slap the shit out of Russell.

"Hell yeah, you been givin' it out for free this long. You might as well put a price on that muthafucka."

Russell reached into his pocket and pulled out a wad of money and held it up in Tianna's face, showing her all the bills. He watched as her eyes got wide, and he knew he'd just reeled her in.

"You see this? I made this shit in one week, spreading my knowledge and taking care of girls just like you. You could be makin' this too, just by layin' on yo back or getting' on yo knees. You young and tight, niggas will pay big money for you."

Tianna thought for a minute as she stared at the money in Russell's hand. Money signs started invading her mind, as she thought about all the new things she could buy with the fast money. This could possibly be the lick she was looking for that could change her life forever.

"So, how much you think I can make?" She asked quickly, eagerness in her tone.

Russell looked at her tight, shapely body and short, blonde pixie cut. Tianna stood about five two, with thick hips and ass, and perfect perky C cup breasts. At eighteen with no kids, her body was perfect, and Russell knew the niggas would pay big for her. Although she was black, her butter pecan colored skin and hazel eyes gave her an exotic look, and he knew he could sale that.

"About twelve hundred a week," he replied.

That was a lot of money. Tianna started to do the math in her head. She figured if she worked with Russell for a year, she would be able to purchase her clothing store and become her own boss. It had been her dream for as long as Tianna could remember to own her own boutique. She knew it would take years to save up for it working at McDonald's. She could save for a decade and still not have enough with the pennies she made there.

"When can I start?" Tianna asked.

Russell smiled because that hadn't taken nearly as much convincing as he thought it would. It was almost too easy, like taking candy from a baby.

"Don't go to work in the mornin'. I'll be back over here in a few hours and we can take some pictures of you to post on my site. After I post them, you should be getting' to work within an hour. That shit don't take long at all."

Tianna nodded her head in understanding, eager to see how the money would start rolling in. She'd never thought she would be selling sex on the internet, but there was no way Tianna could pass up that type of money. Tianna would damn near sale her soul to make enough money to start her own business. Although she didn't realize it, in a way, she was.

"Get you some rest, my baby, you gonna need it, cuz it's gonna be a long night. And that shit smell like money," Russell said, rubbing his hands together while smiling.

Russell walked out the door and Tianna got in bed. She set her alarm for midnight, knowing that Russell would be returning around that time. She fell asleep with money on her mind, feeling as though her hustle was just about to begin.

When her clock alarmed at midnight, Tianna rushed to get into the shower. She knew Russell was on his way, and she didn't want to keep him waiting. She quickly showered and rubbed shea butter all over her body before putting on her robe. There was a knock on the door, and she rushed to it, knowing exactly who it was.

"I brought you somethin' sexy to take pictures in," Russell announced. Holding up a red lace pantie and bra set.

Tianna took the lingerie from his hand and went to the bathroom to put them on. She looked at herself in the mirror and knew that a red lip and a set of false lashes would set the look off. She made her way to her vanity and took a seat, ready to complete the look. When she walked back out to the living room with Russell, he smiled at her beauty. Standing to his feet, he removed his phone from his pocket.

Tianna posed several different ways as Russell snapped shot after shot. Russell directed her on different sexier poses for him to snap, telling her to lean against the couch with her leg up. Or squat down with her legs spread and her tongue out. Tianna obliged without protest, doing everything Russell said. When they were done, he picked her four best pictures to post. No sooner than Tianna changed out of the lingerie did Russell tell her she had a date.

"He wants head and pussy, and you gonna make one fifty off the deal," Russell informed.

"Cool, where is this going down at?" Tianna asked.

"We gonna meet him at a room. Go get changed and put on something sexy. Meet me at my truck when you done," Russell spoke, grabbing his keys from Tianna's coffee table.

When they made it to the motel, Russell told Tianna to stay in the car while he went and collected the money. Russell had a strict policy and let all the men know that nothing went down until all the money was in his hand. The man opened the room door and Russell stepped inside. He looked around the room, and in the bathroom, making sure nobody else was inside the room. Russell had only given the john the price for one person and wanted to make sure he wasn't getting played. Once he was sure no one else other than the man was inside, Russell collected four hundred and fifty dollars from him, then walked back out to the car.

"He's ready for you," Russell stated, and Tianna got out of the car.

She walked up to the motel room door and smiled when she saw the man standing on the other side. He was a tall white man who seemed to be in his mid to late forties. He was handsome, with dark brown hair and brown eyes. She could tell he worked out by his washboard stomach. She was happy that he wasn't ugly and fat.

"Hello there," Tianna greeted, as she closed the door behind her.

"Wow, you are absolutely beautiful. What is your name?" He asked.

Tianna though for a moment, cussing herself for not thinking of a name before she got there. Knowing she wasn't going to give her government name; she said the first thing that came to mind.

"You can call me Amber," Tianna replied, as she walked closer to the man.

She slowly began unbuttoning his shirt, revealing his carved chest. Once his shirt was off, she unbuckled his belt and allowed his pants to drop to the floor. She could see his erect manhood standing at attention through his black silk boxers. Tianna was just about to pull them down when he stopped her.

"I paid for you, so let me do this how I want to," He whispered.

Tianna obliged and allowed the man to take control. He pulled Tianna's tight black dress off her and revealed her naked body. The man licked his lips as he stared at Tianna. Bringing her over to the bed, he laid her down and buried his face between her thick thighs. Tianna moaned as the man's wet tongue gave her more pleasure than she'd ever had. When he was done, he placed a condom on his penis and climbed on top of her. Tianna moaned as he entered her.

For this to be her first time on the job, she was really enjoying this. She wasn't nervous at all like she thought she would be. If every time could be just like this, Tianna was going to love her job. Tianna threw it back and popped her pussy like she had known this man for years. When they were done, Tianna was spent. Naked, she walked into the bathroom to wash the sex from her body. When she returned to the room, her john was already fully dressed and sitting on the bed they had just fucked in.

"Here you go, this is for you," he said, handing her two-hundred-dollar bills.

"Oh, I thought you already paid Russell," Tianna said, confused.

"I did, but I really enjoyed myself with you, so this is your tip," he replied with a wink.

Tianna smiled and placed the money in her bra before thanking him. There was no way she was going to tell Russell about the extra money she'd received. Tianna walked out the room and back to the car with Russell. That's when he informed her that she had another date at the hotel down the street. Tianna smiled and nodded her head as Russell pulled out the parking lot.

Available Now On Amazon

OTHER BOOKS BY

URBAN AINT DEAD

Tales 4rm Da Dale

The Hottest Summer Ever

Hittin' Licks For The Holidays: Atlanta

Wet Dreams On Lockdown: The Nurse

By **Elijah R. Freeman**

Despite The Odds

By **Juhnell Morgan**

Good Girl Gone Rogue

By **Manny Black**

Hittaz

Hittaz 2

Hittaz 3

Hittaz 4

Coldhearted

By **Lou Garden Price, Sr.**

Charge It To The Game

Charge It To The Game 2

A Summer To Remember With My Hitta

Snatched Up By A Hitta

Santa Sent Me A Real One For Christmas

Wet Dreams on Lockdown: The Unit Manager

By **Nai**

A Setup For Revenge

Wet Dreams On Lockdown: The Librarian

By **Ashley Williams**

Ridin' For You

Trickin' on a Heaux for Christmas: A BBW Love Story

Homie Hoppin' For The Holidays

Wet Dreams on Lockdown: The Female C.O

By **Telia Teanna**

The State's Witness

The State's Witness 2

The State's Witness 3

By **Kyiris Ashley**

Stuck In The Trenches

Stuck In The Trenches 2

By **Huff Tha Great**

The Swipe

By **Toōla**

Melted the Heart of a Menace

Wet Dreams On Lockdown: Lieutenant Grace

By P. Wise

Merry Trapmas: Ice & Frost

By **Mia Sky**

Thug Me The Right Way

By **DiamondATL & Nai**

Wet Dreams on Lockdown: The Male C.O

By **Tamyra Griffin**

Wet Dreams On Lockdown: The Counselor

By **Paris Iman**

Wet Dreams On Lockdown: The Warden

By **Shawnice**

Wet Dreams On Lockdown: The Captain

By **TN Jones**

Coming Soon From
<u>URBAN AINT DEAD</u>

The Hottest Summer Ever 2
THE G-CODE
How To Publish A Book From Prison
Tales 4rm Da Dale 2
By **Elijah R. Freeman**

Hittaz 5
Coldhearted 2
By **Lou Garden Price, Sr.**

The Swipe 2
By **Toola**

Good Girls Gone Rogue 2
By **Manny Black**

Despite The Odds 2
Hittin' Licks For The Holidays: Chicago
By **Juhnell Morgan**

Charge It To The Game 3
By **Nai**

Ridin For You, Too
By **Telia Teanna**

A Setup For Revenge 2
By **Ashley Williams**

A Gangsta's Last Kiss
By **Mia Sky**

Pretti & The Beast
By **P. Wise**

BOOKS BY

URBAN AINT DEAD's C.E.O

<u>Elijah R. Freeman</u>

Triggadale

Triggadale 2

Triggadale 3

Tales 4rm Da Dale

The Hottest Summer Ever

Murda Was The Case

Murda Was The Case 2

Murda Was The Case 3

Hittin' Licks For The Holidays: Atlanta

Wet Dreams On Lockdown: The Nurse

STAY CONNECTED

Follow
Elijah R. Freeman
On Social Media
FB: Elijah R. Freeman
IG: @the_future_of_urban_fiction

www.ingramcontent.com/pod-product-compliance
Lightning Source LLC
Chambersburg PA
CBHW072127300726
48975CB00003B/952